The Secret in the Dorm Attic

Jean F. Andrews

Kendall Green Publications
Gallaudet University Press
Washington, D.C.

Kendall Green Publications
An imprint of Gallaudet University Press
Washington, D.C. 20002

Library of Congress Cataloging-in-Publication Data

Andrews, Jean F.
  The secret in the dorm attic.

  Summary: While visiting his friend Matt on the
campus of his special school for the deaf, nine-year-old
Donald discovers something strange going on in the
attic of Matt's dorm and becomes involved in the theft
of a priceless necklace from a nearby museum.
  [1. Deaf—Fiction. 2. Physically handicapped—
Fiction. 3. Schools—Fiction. 4. Mystery and
detective stories] I. Title.
PZ7.A56725Se   1990   [Fic]   90-2972
ISBN 0-930323-66-1

CONTENTS

To Qaisar and Ron

1
SUSAN'S PLANS

"**D**onald, how do I make the sign for *important?*"

Susan Dunbar sat at the kitchen table with a sign language book propped against the sugar jar. It was late August in Kentucky and the weather was hot and humid. Susan was struggling to imitate the manual signs from picture drawings in the book.

"Dang!" she exclaimed. "How can I do anything around here with all these flies?" She banged her book on the table, aiming at a big, black fly.

"Gee whiz," exclaimed Donald getting exasperated with his sister. He turned away from the microwave oven where he was waiting for his popcorn to pop. "Don't you know that yet? Here's how you make that sign. Like this," he said as he demonstrated the correct handshape and movement. Even though Donald was annoyed with Susan, he was secretly pleased that he knew how to do something that his older sister didn't know how to do.

Susan gave Donald a superior look. Swish, swish

went her red ponytail. Usually Susan, who was eleven years old, would not tolerate such disrespect from her nine-year-old brother. She was the brain of the family and always got straight As, unlike Donald who was a slower student. Yet, in spite of having a learning disability, Donald had quickly become fluent in sign language. His best friend Matt, a deaf boy who lived in their neighborhood, had taught him.

Susan was going to give a demonstration to her Girl Scout troop about sign language and she desperately wanted her brother's help right now. "Oh, never mind," she said abruptly. "I will figure out the rest of the signs by myself from the book."

"If you can stop using it as a fly swatter," said Donald sarcastically.

Susan made a face at her brother.

Sign language had become important to Susan after Donald and Matt had started The Flying Fingers Club. The club's purpose was to solve mysteries, and Donald, Matt, and Susan made up the sleuthing trio.

"I wish Matt were here," Susan said. "I just can't read these pictures of signs," she continued as she tried to get her brother's help without having to ask for it. Susan tried another tack. "How am I going to help you and Matt solve more mysteries if I don't know sign language?" she asked as she threw her arms up in a sweeping, dramatic gesture. *That should convince him to help me,* she thought.

Donald's attention was captured by his sister's

moves. "And I want to show the other Scouts next weekend at camp," Susan continued. "Now about these signs—"

"Is something burning?" called the children's father from the dining room. He and his wife were cataloging bags of soils that were spread out over the table. Merlin, the family cat, lay on the floor nearby.

"Oh, Mom, look!" Donald stood in the dining room doorway with the popcorn bag in his hands. He pointed to the mound of black kernels at the bottom of the bag. "Burnt again! Something's wrong with that microwave. Every time I try to make popcorn it just burns up. I don't understand it. I think we should throw out that old thing and get a new one."

"Did you follow the directions, son?" asked his father.

"Of course, Dad. I always do. I mean—I always try to."

"When you burn something, it usually means that you used too much heat or cooked it too long," said his mother as she reached across the table and picked up another bag of soil. "Mmmm—must be a clay mixture," she said. Her attention was off Donald and on her soils again. Donald's mother was a professor of soil science. His father was a computer programmer and he often helped his wife catalog her soil samples on the computer. The family had just returned from a summer trip to the southwestern part of the United States. They had brought back lots of soil samples that Donald's mother planned to use in her classes.

"Well, let me see the bag. Now tell me again. What did you do?" asked his mother.

Donald pushed his glasses back onto his nose. He put the bag on the table and ran both his hands through his short, curly brown hair. "Well, I unfolded the bag and put it in the middle of the microwave just like the picture shows. Then I put it on high, for . . . for . . . let me see. . . . It's hard to read through the burnt bag." Donald leaned over and looked at the bag again. "Oh, here it is. I put the timer on for eight minutes."

"Eight minutes seems too long. Let me see that bag, Donald," said his mother. Specks of black popcorn kernels spilled on the floor. Merlin emerged from under the dining room table and sniffed the charred kernels.

"Donald, I think you misread this," she said.

"Donald misread what?" asked Susan as she suddenly appeared at the door.

"None of your business!" snapped Donald. He was embarrassed and didn't want his sister to tease him.

"Oh, sick, Donald! Burnt popcorn!" exclaimed Susan.

"Donald, the directions say three minutes not eight minutes," explained his mother. "That's why your popcorn is burnt. You have to read the directions carefully."

"Hee, hee!" Susan put her hand over her mouth to muffle a giggle.

4

"Oh, I hate this. They're always trying to trick you," he complained.

"No one is trying to trick you. You just have to watch your numbers, that's all," said his mother as she picked up another bag of soil.

The clang of the mail slot in the front door distracted Susan and Donald from the popcorn mishap. They raced to the front door.

"Donald," said Susan excitedly, "here's a letter for you from Matt!" Donald reached over and grabbed the letter. He tore it open and began to read. "Oh boy, I can go! I can go! It's all set."

"You mean your trip to Matt's school?" asked his mother. The plans had already been discussed with Matt and his mother before the family had gone on vacation. Donald had been waiting to hear from Matt to get the date confirmed.

"Oh, I can't wait!" Donald began to jump up and down. "I get to meet all Matt's friends and stay in the dorm and go to Cumberland Falls with him!"

"Great!" chimed in Susan. "My Girl Scout troop will be camping there the same weekend. We can do all kinds of things together—like play volleyball and tell ghost stories around the camp fire and—"

"Ah, come on, Susan!" Donald interrupted Susan. "The boys plan on going to Cumberland Falls to go hiking and rafting and horseback riding and. . . ."

"But Donald, you can do all that stuff during the day," Susan responded. "Then we can play volleyball and have bonfires at night. You love toasted marshmallows, don't you? It's simply a matter of scheduling. Look, I will make a list."

Susan loved to make lists. And to be boss.

"Hey, don't forget, Matt and I have important business to do before we go to Cumberland Falls. We have to investigate the mysterious trapdoor in the attic of his dorm," said Donald.

"I'm sure the Flying Fingers Club can solve the case," said their father, hoping that his children would stop arguing.

"That's for sure," agreed Mrs. Dunbar.

After Donald and Matt had solved the mystery of Susan's disappearing newspapers, they had reluctantly let Susan join their club. They hated to admit it, but they needed her brains.

"How is Matt liking his school?" their mother asked. "I remember he wasn't very happy last year at Lincoln Elementary."

"Oh, he loves it. He likes being back with his deaf friends." replied Donald. "But I miss him so much," he added quietly and a bit sadly.

The next few days Donald spent deciding what to pack for his trip to Matt's school and the weekend at Cumberland Falls. He stuffed his backpack with several changes of clothes.

"Don't forget your swimsuit and some towels," his mother reminded him.

"And your jackknife and water canteen," said his father. "And that goes for you too, Susan."

The day finally arrived when Donald's parents took him to the bus. Donald was traveling from his home town of Richmond to Danville, 40 miles away, where the Kentucky State School for the Deaf was located.

"I will be seeing you at Cumberland Falls next weekend," said Susan right before Donald got on the bus. "I worked out all the plans. I can't wait to find out what you and Matt discover in the attic."

As the bus rolled out of the station, Donald waved to his family and settled down to read his comic book. He gazed out the window and saw rolling green hills. Several chestnut mares were grazing under a tree near a white fence. Then Donald noticed a strange-looking man sitting in the back of the bus. The man wore a brown felt hat pulled down over his eyes and had a red bandanna tied around his neck. His complexion and hair were dark. And he had a mustache. Donald wondered where this mysterious man was from and where he was going. But the steady hum of the bus soon lulled him to sleep. He laid his head on the cushioned seat and dozed off.

2
A DIFFERENT KIND OF SCHOOL

"**H**ey, kid, I think this is your stop." The bus driver turned around and called to Donald.

Donald sat up straight and rubbed the sleep from his eyes. He looked around and saw several red brick buildings surrounded by trees. *There's Matt. And that must be his dorm counselor*, thought Donald. *There's the Kentucky State School for the Deaf sign Matt told me about.* Donald reached down on the floor and picked up his backpack.

"Hi, Donald!" signed Matt as he saw his friend hop off the bus. Matt was stocky, short, and blond. Next to him stood a tall man in his early thirties. "This is Mr. Benning, my dorm counselor."

Donald shook hands with the tall man. Mr. Benning rapidly signed to Donald but Donald could not understand a word.

Mr. Benning saw the confused expression on Donald's face. He spoke. "Welcome! I'm happy you arrived safely. Let's take your things and go to the dorm now. You don't want to be late for supper." Donald was grateful that the dorm counselor spoke so clearly.

"It will take you awhile to understand the sign we use here. It's a bit different than the sign I used at Lincoln Elementary," Matt explained.

"Why?" Donald wanted to know.

"Because it's deaf sign, not hearing sign."

"Huh? What do you mean?" Donald was even more confused. "You mean you use a different sign with me than you do with your deaf friends?"

"Deaf sign is what I use with my deaf friends. It's called American Sign Language. It's different than the sign most hearing people use. Hearing sign is more like English. Hearing sign is slower. I don't like it as much," Matt explained.

"Do you use deaf sign at home, too?" asked Donald.

"Of course," replied Matt. "My parents are deaf."

"What about Jessie?" Donald asked, referring to Matt's two-year-old hearing sister.

"We use deaf sign with her, too, because she's one of us."

"But she's hearing," replied Donald.

"But she's in our family so we use deaf sign with her. She can sign more than she can talk," continued Matt.

"See you in the cafeteria, boys," Mr. Benning signed and spoke, interrupting the boys' conversation. He rapidly took off across campus.

Matt explained that Mr. Benning could speak so well because he had lost his hearing as an adult. "He's a *great* dorm counselor and teacher," Matt signed with a big grin on his face.

Matt picked up Donald's backpack and they walked across the sidewalk, through a parking lot, and up a small grassy hill toward an old brick building.

"This is my dorm. It's the best one at the school," Matt boasted.

The boys entered the building and climbed a flight of wooden stairs. When they got to the landing, Matt stopped and put Donald's things down on the floor.

"See the old paint chipping away up there?" signed Matt. He pointed to the ceiling. Up on the ceiling was a trapdoor. "Look at those black smudges around it. I think those are someone's fingerprints. And that padlock looks like it's broken. See?"

Donald nodded slowly. Matt had the sharpest eyes of any of his friends. He saw details that most people would overlook.

"We need to climb up there and see what's behind that trapdoor."

"Yeah," replied Donald. He felt a shiver of anticipation go up and down his spine. Donald could smell a mystery here.

The boys entered a large room. On two sides of the room five beds were lined up against the wall. A sofa, several comfortable chairs, and a TV were grouped at the far end of the room.

"Here, take this bed," said Matt to Donald pointing to the bed next to his. "The bathroom is over there." Matt gestured toward an adjoining room.

The students had decorated the walls by their beds with posters of their favorite movie stars and sports heroes. Matt had a picture of Superman on his wall and a Cincinnati Reds pennant on the ceiling over his bed. Different colored spreads and quilts covered the boys' beds, giving the room a cheery appearance.

"Hey, you brought all your blue ribbons for swimming from your room at home," signed Donald, pointing to the wall by Matt's bed.

"I sure did! I'm really proud of them! I'm the number one backstroker in the whole school!" signed Matt, beaming with pride. "I beat everybody in practice last week."

Donald was impressed by Matt's ribbons. He wanted to be a champion at something, too.

Matt went on. "This isn't like my room at home. My room is messier at home. But here we have to clean up every morning. See that list over there?"

Donald nodded.

"That's the work list," signed Matt. "I hate lists!"

"I do, too," replied Donald. "Susan and Mom are always making lists of things I have to do."

Matt laughed. "Yeah, I know how that is. Come on. Let's go see some more of the campus." The boys headed out of the building and across campus. Matt began to explain and describe each of the buildings the boys saw.

"This is our infirmary. The nurses are real nice. They give you ice cream and 7-Up and let you watch TV when you get sick."

"It's just like a little hospital," Donald replied.

"And there are the classrooms." Matt pointed to another building. "We will go to classes tomorrow. My favorite class is science. We have an aquarium . with fish and two cages of gerbils." Matt continued the tour. "And over here is the gym. We have a basketball court, wrestling mats, and a big swimming pool with a diving board!" Matt signed to Donald. "I can do a flip off the high board," Matt bragged. "Can you?"

"Uh, I don't think so," answered Donald. "I'm afraid of heights."

"It's easy!" Matt signed. "I can teach you! And I will show you how to do the backstroke real fast."

"This is really great!" Donald was impressed by Matt's school. Not only was it bigger than Lincoln Elementary, but it had all sorts of other facilities. "I wish my school had all these things."

"Yeah, but I still miss being at home. I even miss Jessie." Matt looked sad. "Even though she always gets into my toys and makes a mess of my room. Right before I left for school, Jessie took a bite out of my favorite rubber dinosaur! I was so mad!"

"Remember when she scribbled all over our new comic books?" asked Donald.

"Yeah," laughed Matt. "I can't wait until she gets older. Then maybe she will do something useful like answer the phone, instead of making a pest out of herself!"

The boys were now behind the dorms. A big

pond surrounded by marshy grass was in front of them. Mosquitoes buzzed in the air.

"That's Catfish Pond," Matt explained. He swatted a big mosquito on his leg. "People from town can fish there if they want to. See? Like that man and boy over there."

Donald stopped and looked again. "That man was on the bus with me," he signed to Matt.

"The man and the boy kind of look alike," observed Matt. "Their skin color is the same and their hair color, too. They're both dark. Do you think they're related?"

"I don't know," answered Donald.

Then something peculiar happened. The boy handed the man a note. The man read it, wrote something, and returned it to him. While the boy read the note, the man threw pebbles into the pond.

"I wonder what that's all about?" signed Matt. "I have never seen either of those people before."

"Well, the man just came to town," replied Donald. "He looks like he's from a foreign country. I don't know where, though."

"Maybe India," answered Matt. "Look, the boy is using sign language. He must be deaf."

"Does he go to school here?" Donald asked.

"If he does, I haven't seen him before," replied Matt. "Maybe he just arrived, like you did."

The boys' conversation was interrupted by a group of other boys coming toward them.

"Oh, here come my friends." As the boys circled around Matt and Donald, Matt began the introductions. "This is my hearing friend, Donald. His name sign is —." Matt made a D-handshape on his left shoulder.

The boys nodded and smiled at Donald and then began to sign rapidly to each other. Matt joined in their conversation. The boys started laughing and joking.

There they go again, thought Donald. *Using that stupid old deaf sign. I can't understand it at all. Everyone's talking about me and laughing at me!* Donald's face turned bright red. He folded his arms across his chest and began to pout.

Matt, noticing his friend's change of attitude, turned to him. "What's the matter, Donald? You feeling okay?" he asked innocently.

"I don't understand what everyone is signing," Donald signed angrily. "You're ignoring me. I hate that!"

"Now you see how it feels," replied Matt. "When you're talking to your hearing friends, I get left out."

"That's not true!" Donald retorted, shaking his head. "I always interpret for you."

"Not always!" Matt was becoming angry, too. "Only sometimes. Anyway, we're not talking about you. I just haven't seen my deaf friends all summer. We're catching up on news, that's all."

One boy, sensing the rising tension between Donald and Matt, signed to Donald. "Do you want to play baseball with us after dinner?" Donald thought he understood.

"It's like I told you, Donald," signed Matt

impatiently. "We sign much faster here and use deaf sign. You will pick it up fast. Ask Ted. He knows." Matt pointed to the boy who had asked Donald to play baseball with them.

"Yes," volunteered Ted. "My sister is hearing. She's slow at reading my signs, but she improves when I go home and she can practice with me. Same with you."

"I think I understand some," signed Donald.

"Don't worry," Ted reassured Donald. "We'll help you out."

But not all the boys were as friendly as Ted. Several just stood with their arms across their chests and stared at Donald.

"Why did you bring that dumb-looking hearing boy here?" one big boy named Larry asked.

"Yeah," added another boy. "We don't want any hearing kids in our school."

"He's visiting, that's all," replied Matt. Quickly changing the subject, he signed, "I'm hungry. Let's go to the cafeteria," and motioned to everyone.

"Don't worry, Donald," Matt consoled. "Larry and the others will warm up later. They're just not used to hearing people, that's all."

But Matt's reassurance did not comfort Donald. He had felt real hostility from some of the boys and he did not like it one bit. Maybe it was not such a good idea for him to come visit Matt after all.

In the cafeteria, the boys stood in the food line. Larry suddenly shoved Donald against the wall.

"Hey! Cut it out!" shouted Donald. He punched Larry in the shoulder.

"Oh, excuse me, big shot." Larry signed slowly. Then Larry shoved Donald against the wall again. Donald fell in a heap on the floor. Slowly he got up and raised his fists.

Mr. Benning was watching the boys from the other side of the cafeteria. He came over and took Larry and Donald aside. "Look, I don't know who started this fight but it has got to stop. You boys are here to eat—not fight," he signed sternly.

"But . . . but . . .," Donald blurted out, "I didn't start it!"

Larry shrugged his shoulders and signed. "I was just standing in line minding my own business and. . . ."

"Okay, you boys. Enough is enough. I don't want to know anymore. Just get back in line and you better get along with each other or you will spend the rest of the evening in the dorm."

"Donald," Matt tried to comfort his friend, "just forget it. Larry is always picking fights with kids here. Look at the food. Choose what you want."

"I'm not hungry anymore," Donald replied angrily. "I just want to go home! It's not fair here."

"Donald, just ignore Larry. It will be okay. Besides, he's a lousy baseball player. We will get him back on the baseball field later."

The mention of revenge made Donald feel better. His bad mood began to dissolve and his attention went back to more important matters—such as food.

"Grab a tray," instructed Matt.

"Can you eat as much as you want?" asked Donald.

"Sure," answered Matt. "And we can choose what we want for all three meals."

"Hey, Matt. Have you met that new boy yet?" interrupted Ted.

Matt shook his head.

"He looks like he's from a foreign country or something," Ted signed.

"And there he is!" Another boy in the food line who had been watching the boys' conversation pointed toward the new student.

Matt and Donald looked at each other and nodded, recognizing the boy they had seen by the pond.

3

SALEEM

"**W**hat's your name and where are you from?" Ted asked.

"My name is Saleem and I'm from Pakistan," the boy answered shyly. Saleem was tall and slender with wavy, jet-black hair and an olive complexion. He wore a T-shirt and blue jeans with high-top sneakers like the other boys. Several boys and girls had gathered around him in the food line. Saleem's signs were clear and his fingerspelling was easy to read.

Even though their teachers had informed them that a new boy from a foreign country would be attending the school, the kids were still apprehensive. Bluntly, they began asking questions.

"Are you a black person?" asked one boy.

"No," answered Saleem. "I'm from Pakistan. It's next to India."

"How did you learn to sign?"

"I spent last summer in a camp for deaf kids in Minnesota," replied Saleem. "That's where I learned signs and fingerspelling."

18

"Then why are you here in Kentucky?" asked a girl.

"My Aunt Saba and Uncle Bill are history professors at the College here," he answered. "We don't have many good schools for the deaf in Pakistan, so my aunt and uncle thought I should go here for a while to get a better education."

"So you live with your aunt and uncle?" asked another boy.

"On weekends. But I will live here in the dorm during the week so I can play baseball and join in other activities."

"Hey, kids! Keep this line moving," motioned one of the dorm counselors. Saleem found a place in line right in front of Donald. Steam rose from metal bins of beans and hot dogs. Plates of cole slaw, lime jello, and crumb cake were on the side. Cartons of cold milk were stacked at the end of the serving counter.

Saleem shook his head *no* when the lady gestured, asking him if he wanted hot dogs.

"You must be crazy!" signed Matt. "Those hot dogs are really good. I usually eat three or four."

"I can't eat hot dogs," signed Saleem. "Or bacon or sausage or any pork. It's forbidden by my religion." Matt and Donald looked at each other. They had never heard anything like that before.

"What a weirdo!" signed one boy who was watching the conversation.

"Come over and eat with us," Matt invited Saleem. The boys found three empty seats at a table.

"You're only going to eat your cole slaw, beans, jello, and crumb cake?" asked Matt.

Saleem nodded as he heaped cole slaw on his fork.

Donald sat quietly. He was still having trouble understanding the signs. *Everyone here signs so fast!* he thought to himself.

"Yeah, but don't worry about me not eating those hot dogs," Saleem signed. "I have some goodies stashed away in my footlocker in the dorm."

"What kind of goodies?" asked Matt smacking his lips. He thought of his mother's packages filled with chocolate chip cookies and other favorite sweets.

"Aunt Saba fixes me *gajer ka Halwva*," he explained to the curious boys.

"What's that?" asked Matt.

"Oh, it's a sweet carrot cake with almonds in it," answered Saleem. "I will let you try some later if you like."

"I will try it," decided Matt. Matt turned to Donald and fingerspelled "carrot cake" slowly so that Donald could understand. Donald decided he would pass. Carrot cake did not sound appealing to him.

"Hey, do you want to play baseball?" asked Ted on his way out of the cafeteria.

Matt opened his mouth and stuck out his tongue, green from the jello he was eating.

"Yuk!" replied Ted. "I guess that means *yes*." The boys laughed.

"Do we have to let that foreign weirdo and that dumb hearing boy play with us?" asked Larry. "Who wants them anyhow?"

"Let them play! We need more players. It's more fun that way." Ted stuck up for Saleem and Donald.

Larry shrugged his shoulders and glared at Saleem and Donald.

Donald was first at bat. Even though he loved baseball, he was not very good at it. "Strike one!" motioned the pitcher after the first ball sailed over the plate and Donald tried unsuccessfully to hit it.

Another pitch whizzed by. "Strike two!"

"Strike three and you're out!" signed the pitcher. Donald was disappointed. No matter how hard he tried he always had trouble hitting the ball.

Next, Matt stepped to the plate and hit a grounder deep into left field. He slid into second base for an easy double.

When Saleem came up to bat, no one expected him to make a hit. *Crack!* The ball soared out of the playing field and into the road.

The pitcher threw up his arms in amazement. "I've never seen anyone hit the ball that far!"

Matt ran to home plate and Saleem sped around the three bases and into home.

The boys played until dark. Donald and Saleem were not spared teasing from some of the bigger boys.

"Come on in," motioned Mr. Benning. He had noticed that some of the boys were unfriendly towards Saleem and Donald. "You boys have school tomorrow so you have to shower and turn in early. No TV tonight."

"Aw!" Several boys whined and complained.

On the stairs, Matt turned to Saleem. "Where did you learn to hit the ball like that?"

"My Uncle Bill taught me," answered Saleem. "He played baseball when he was in college. He was real good. It's mostly how you grip the bat and swing into the ball. Here, I will show you." Saleem picked up a broom that was in the corner of the dorm room and demonstrated the grip to Matt. He swung the broom without looking behind him. The broom whacked several boys in the face.

"Hey, watch what you're doing," one of the boys protested.

"Yeah, you want to fight?" another boy asked angrily.

"Look, he didn't mean it." Matt was trying to avoid a fight. "Saleem was just showing me something."

"Sure," answered Larry with a sneer on his face. "Foreigners are all alike. You just can't trust any of them."

Now Matt was boiling mad. "Knock it off!" Matt signed to Larry, scowling at him.

Larry grabbed his towel, snapped it at Matt's legs, and ran into the bathroom.

Matt ignored Larry's attack. His thoughts were on Saleem. *How athletic Saleem is*, Matt thought. *He can really smack a baseball. Maybe I can learn to do that, too. And what was he doing with that strange man by the pond?* Matt wondered.

Matt gestured to Saleem and Donald to follow him into the hall. He didn't want anyone else to see their conversation. "Who was that man you were talking to this afternoon at the pond? The one with the brown hat and red bandanna?" Matt asked.

"Oh, that was Abdul," replied Saleem. "He's the new janitor. He just started working here."

"What did he want from you," asked Matt.

"I'm not real sure. He asked me all sorts of questions," answered Saleem. He doesn't know sign language and I couldn't speechread him very well because of his moustache, so we wrote notes back and forth. See?" Saleem pulled a note out of his pocket and showed it to the boys.

Looking at the Arabic letters, Donald thought how strange this note was. Matt, too, was puzzled by the writing.

"What's that? A secret code?" asked Donald.

Saleem laughed. "No, the note is written in Urdu, the language of my people in Pakistan. It's much different than English."

Matt and Donald peered closely at the note. The letters were made with broad strokes.

Saleem went on. "Abdul is from Afghanistan, a country near Pakistan," he signed.

"What did he want?" asked Matt.

"He wanted to know about some room up above the ceiling here," answered Saleem.

Matt and Donald looked at each other knowingly. "Attic," Donald said and Matt signed.

"But I told him I didn't know anything about the attic because I just moved into the dorm myself." Saleem had already picked up the sign for *attic*.

Donald heard noises that sounded like something heavy being dragged across the floor. He motioned to Matt and Saleem and they followed him into the dorm room. Saleem's belongings and Donald's backpack were piled on Matt's bed. Saleem's footlocker was near the end of Matt's bed.

Several of the boys were standing with their arms folded across their chests and angry expressions on their faces.

"This is *our* dorm. It's not for hearing kids or foreigners. We want those two out of here. *Now!*" signed Larry.

4

ROOMMATE PROBLEMS

"**W**hat's going on? What do you mean?" Matt asked angrily. Several of the boys circled around Matt.

"He's just a foreigner," signed Larry.

"Yeah, he looks weird," added another.

"And look at all that junk he keeps in his footlocker."

"We don't like that flag he has hanging over his bed, either. Maybe he's a spy!"

"He's new," signed Matt slowly. He was feeling the hostility of the group. It gave him a creepy feeling and he was scared. "You just have to give him a chance," he added, looking around the room cautiously. Matt knew he was outnumbered.

"We don't want your hearing friend here, either," signed Larry. "This dorm is for deaf only!"

"Come on, Matt," Ted signed. "You can understand our feelings. We just want this room to be for people like us."

The boys stamped their feet. *"Deaf only! Deaf only! No foreigners!"* The boys moved over to a side wall leaving Matt, Donald, and Saleem standing in the middle of the room.

Matt was surprised that Ted had joined the other boys against Saleem and Donald. Matt's anger overcame his fear. "This is *my* room, too! And I can invite anyone I want to stay with me. You're just sore because our team beat you in baseball. Saleem can hit the ball harder and farther than any of you and you're all jealous!" signed Matt aggressively. "I think you're all—I think you're all *stupid*!" Matt was so angry that his fist made a red spot on his forehead where he made the sign for *stupid*.

"Hey, big shot! Watch who you call stupid!" Larry signed as he moved toward Matt. He grabbed Matt and wrestled him to the ground. On the sidelines, the other boys started to cheer as the wrestlers rolled across the floor.

Crash! Matt's leg got caught in the wire of the floor lamp and it fell to the floor.

Boom! The boys rolled into a bookcase and a shelfful of paperbacks tumbled down to the ground.

"Go, Matt!" cheered Donald. "Kill him!" Saleem jumped up and down excitedly.

"Get him! Get him!" shouted another boy pointing to Matt.

The boys rolled over and over on the floor. Matt struggled to break the headlock Larry had on him.

Suddenly, the lights in the room flicked on and off.

"Hey! What's going on in here?" Mr. Benning stood in the doorway, a scowl on his face. "That's enough! Stop! I thought I told you boys to get ready for bed!"

The boys stopped fighting and stood up.

"Who started this?" asked Mr. Benning calmly. "I suspect it has something to do with our two visitors. Come on, guys," he signed with a pleading look on his face, "let's show some hospitality around here."

Nobody answered the dorm counselor. The boys hung their heads shamefully. When they looked up, Mr. Benning continued. "Finish showering and get into bed. Lights out in fifteen minutes." He left the room.

"You sleep on that side. We're moving our beds away from you," sneered one boy. "We don't want your cooties."

"That's fine with us," replied Matt. "We don't want your cooties, either!"

The boys settled down and began preparing for bed.

"Hey, Matt," signed Donald, "I think I'm getting the hang of your deaf sign. I understood almost everything that happened." Donald was feeling very proud of himself.

After the boys had finished showering and had gotten into bed, it was quiet in the dorm. Matt turned to Donald and Saleem and signed something in the moonlight that was filtering in through the window. The three boys giggled.

"Okay," signed Matt. "I will give the signal."

Ten minutes later, the boys slipped out of bed and picked up their pillows. *Wham! Wham!* The soft pillows fell on the bodies of the other boys.

"Ahhhh!" shouted Matt.

"Surprise attack!" Donald yelled.

In less than a minute, all the boys were swatting each other with pillows. Matt stood on his bed and swung his pillow. *Whomp!* The boys raced around the room trying to clobber each other. Several boys used their beds as trampolines and began doing somersaults.

"We're winning!" shouted Donald.

"Yayyyy!" Saleem yelled.

A boy hit Saleem in the stomach with his pillow and Saleem fell laughing on his bed. The pillow fell out of its pillowcase. It split open and hundreds of wispy white feathers flew into the air. Soon, thousands of feathers swirled around the room.

"It's snowing in August in Kentucky," signed Ted, laughing gleefully.

A boy ran over to the sofa and pulled off a cushion. *Whomp!* He heaved it across the room and it landed on Ted.

"Hey, no fair," complained Ted. "Those cushions are too hard!"

The lights flicked on and off. By the doorway stood Mr. Benning with his arms folded and a stern expression on his face.

"I'm glad you all decided to get along with each other now," he signed, pleased to see the friendly ruckus rather than the angry fighting he had seen earlier. "But this has got to stop! Now clean up this mess." Emphatically he added, *"Right now!"*

28

For the next half hour, the boys swept the dorm floor and cleaned up feathers.

"It's all Saleem and Donald's fault," one boy complained. "If they hadn't come here, we never would have been fighting. They should have to clean up this mess, not us."

"Oh, drop dead!" signed Matt. "You all started the fight and you know it."

"Good night, boys!" Mr. Benning stood by the door and motioned the boys to get into bed. "Sleep well."

After all the commotion, the tired boys quickly fell into sound sleep. Everyone, that is, except Donald. He could not sleep.

He turned his head and looked out the window. It was a quiet, moonlit night. His eyes wandered back into the room and he stared up at the ceiling, watching a moth fly around in the corner. Thoughts whirled around in Donald's head. *A lot has happened since I left home. Matt's school is different. It's a lot bigger than Lincoln. Staying in the dorm is kind of fun. I have a new friend, Saleem. I think I'm beginning to understand deaf sign. Who's this strange man Abdul? Why did he want to know about the attic?* After awhile, Donald's mind quit racing. Just when he was about to doze off, he heard a loud noise!

Up above in the attic, Abdul sat in a corner eating crackers and sardines. He and another janitor had been in and out of the attic all afternoon, clearing it out. He had sneaked back in just before the boys came in from playing baseball. He needed to check out a few things. Abdul shone his flashlight into each corner of the attic and found books, scraps of paper, and old pieces of furniture. He leaned down and brushed some cobwebs from an old painting propped against the wall, scraping his hand across a nail protruding from the wooden picture frame.

"Ow!" he exclaimed as he brought his injured hand to his mouth. The flashlight dropped from his grasp, clunked loudly to the floor, and rolled into the corner. Blood oozed from his hand and down his wrist. The pain quickly subsided. He picked the picture up and examined it. The back came away easily, revealing a one-inch gap between the picture itself and the back of the frame. Abdul smiled and muttered to himself, "This will be perfect!"

What Donald had heard was the *clunk* of the flashlight. He sat up abruptly, leaned across his bed, and shook Matt.

Matt rubbed the sleep from his eyes and looked at Donald questioningly.

"I heard a noise," signed Donald. "And I think it came from the attic!"

5

NOISES IN THE ATTIC

Donald and Matt slipped out of bed. Matt got his flashlight from his top dresser drawer and then motioned for Donald to follow him.

Saleem touched Donald's shoulder and signed, "I want to come, too."

"Put your blankets under the sheets," Matt ordered. "That way, when Mr. Benning checks our beds, it will look like we're asleep." Saleem and Donald followed Matt's instructions. Then the three boys headed for the hallway.

"Hey, look!" Matt pointed to the trapdoor. "It looks like a light is on up there. See through that crack?"

"Yeah," Donald answered. "Do you think it's safe to go up there? Maybe someone will slug us or something. Maybe we should go up another time?"

"I think we should go back to bed," signed Saleem. "This looks too dangerous."

"But, Donald," Matt protested, "we have to investigate. Something strange is going on around here and we have to get to the bottom of it." Matt knew exactly what he was going to do. He was going to explore the attic! "Wait here. I will go get the ladder."

In a few minutes, Matt was back with a ladder. He climbed up first. The metal latch had already been unfastened so he gently pushed the wooden trapdoor up and over to the side. Matt peered inside, then hoisted himself up into the attic room. He motioned to Saleem and Donald, who were standing at the bottom of the ladder, to follow him.

The boys were right under the roof of the dorm. The ceiling came to a point and the walls slanted down. The boys crouched on their knees and looked around.

"Hey, I can't breathe up here." Saleem was coughing. "My allergies," he complained.

Big black cockroaches scurried across the floor. A powerful flashlight lay in the corner and lit up the attic.

"Let's close this trapdoor just a bit," Matt signed. "When Mr. Benning comes by to check on us, he might notice the light. It's bad enough we left the ladder down there."

"Good idea," Donald answered. So the boys gently closed the trapdoor, putting a small piece of wood under it so that it would not close completely.

"Hey, look at all the neat junk up here," Matt signed.

On one side of the room was an old oil painting of a man. Crawling on his knees over to the painting, Matt wiped off some of the dust. "I wonder who this is?" he asked. "Somebody famous, I bet. I would like to take it down and hang it by my bed."

"It sure smells up here." Saleem wrinkled his nose in distaste. "Seems like it hasn't been cleaned in years."

"Look at all those books," signed Donald. "I bet they're a hundred years old. And the furniture! Look at the old-fashioned school desks. This must be a storage room for all the school's old things."

"Ahhh!" yelled Saleem. "I almost stepped on a mousetrap. I could have lost all my toes!" He began to cry softly.

"Oh, don't be such a wimp," signed Matt impatiently. "It would only pinch you a bit."

Towards the back of the attic was a small shelf below a square window. The window was slightly open. A gust of wind blew into the attic. Suddenly, the flashlight that had been left on the floor went dead.

"I can't see!" yelled Donald. Saleem grabbed Matt's arm.

Matt flicked on his flashlight. "There. That helps some. Here, Saleem," Matt offered, "take my flashlight and look around a bit. That will stop you being such a scaredy-cat!"

Suddenly, Donald heard a screeching sound. A flap of wings followed the eerie noise and a pair of bats swooped over the boys' heads and flew out the window.

"Whew!" Donald heaved a sigh of relief. "It's only bats."

"Only bats!" Saleem replied. "They could bite us!"

"Oh, no," explained Donald. "Bats are nice animals. They eat lots of bugs and stuff like that. They won't hurt you."

Saleem had been shining the flashlight around the room. Suddenly, he got very excited. "Look at that!" Saleem pointed to an empty sardine tin and a box of crackers. Donald opened the crackers and ate one.

"Donald," warned Matt, "this is no time for a snack. That food might be rotten."

"I'm gathering evidence," Donald signed. "These crackers are still crisp. That means that someone has been here recently." Donald was feeling smug. He'd gotten to eat a cracker *and* point out a clue.

"We knew that," signed Matt, "because of the noise and the flashlight."

"Yeah, but it never hurts to get more evidence," Donald added, still satisfied with himself.

"Do you think Abdul has been up here?" asked Saleem. "He asked me about this place, remember? I told you about our conversation by the pond."

"But why would he want to come up here when he has an apartment on campus like the other janitors?" Matt asked.

"Maybe the others don't like him," answered Saleem slowly. "It's hard coming from another country. People don't accept you very easily." His head dropped down.

"But why would he pick our dorm?" Matt continued.

The boys were stumped. Donald quickly turned around. "I heard something," he signed.

"What? What is it?"

Donald turned toward the trapdoor. The wood piece had been removed and the trapdoor slammed shut.

"Oh, no!" exclaimed Donald. "Someone has shut the trapdoor!"

Matt tugged at the handle of the trapdoor. "It's stuck! I can't open it!"

"Here, let me try," signed Donald. He tried to open the wooden door, but it would not move.

"What are we going to do?" Saleem asked desperately. "I wish I had never come with you guys. We might die up here!" He began to cry.

"Saleem," signed Donald with his teeth clenched, "stop being such a crybaby! You have been complaining since you got here. Just shut up! We will get out of here!" Donald was panicked, too, and felt like crying. But he didn't.

The three boys sat on the dirty floor near the trapdoor. Nobody moved. Suddenly, Donald reached into his pocket and pulled out his jackknife. He tried to pry open the wooden door.

"I can't get it open!" said Donald, desperately, shaking his head. "It won't budge!"

The three boys sat quietly in the moonlight coming in from the window. Saleem clutched the flashlight. "I hear a squeak over by the window," signed Donald to Saleem and Matt. "I think it's one of the bats."

Saleem shone the flashlight towards the window. By the side of the wall was a tiny brown bat caught in an old fishing net.

"We shouldn't touch it," Matt warned. "It might have rabies."

"If it's a healthy bat, it won't have rabies," answered Donald. "We should free it."

"No way," Saleem answered emphatically. "I'm not touching any bat, not for a million dollars!"

"We don't have to touch it," replied Donald calmly. "Just shake it loose from the net so it can fly away." Matt and Donald picked up the net and carefully carried it to the window. They dropped the net through the crack in the window and shook it. The bat squealed and flew up into the sky.

"Look at that pine tree. That big branch almost touches the side of the building," signed Matt excitedly. "If we can get out this window, we can climb down the tree."

"You guys must be crazy!" signed Saleem.

The other two boys looked at Saleem and shrugged.

In no time at all, Donald and Matt had opened the window. One at a time, the three boys climbed out onto the branch and down the tree. The boys landed safely on the ground. Donald and Matt had big grins on their faces.

"Oh, yuk! I'm all dirty," Saleem complained.

"Look," Matt signed, pointing to a low branch.

"There's something caught in the tree. It's a red bandanna!"

"It looks like the one Abdul wears around his neck all the time," signed Donald.

"But why is it here? What's going on?" signed Matt as he stuffed the bandanna into his back pocket.

The boys were puzzled.

Suddenly a tall dark shape emerged from behind a nearby bush.

"Ahhh!" screamed Saleem, terrified. Donald and Matt closed their eyes. The shadow came closer and closer to the boys until it stood in a pool of moonlight.

"Out for a midnight stroll, boys?"

"Mr. Benning!" Donald cried out.

"You scared us!" signed Saleem.

"Get in your beds right now!" Mr. Benning signed with a stern expression on his face. "And tomorrow morning you have a lot of explaining to do!"

6
THE BATTLE

"**W**e sure got off easy this morning," signed Matt to Donald. "Whew!"

"Yeah, but I still feel bad that we told a lie," replied Donald.

"It wasn't all that bad," signed Matt. "After all, Saleem does have allergies. And he does have to go out and get fresh air now and then so he can breathe better. We just changed the details, that's all. And about the ladder in the hallway—well, we did want to make sure all the feathers were cleaned off the tops of those tall windows in our room."

"Do you think Mr. Benning fell for our alibi? That the reason we were all outside was for Saleem's sake?" asked Donald.

"I think he did. If he knew we were up in the attic, he would have said that the attic was off limits," replied Matt.

Donald nodded. "Who do you think shut the trapdoor on us? Do you think it was Larry?"

"I doubt it," replied Matt thoughtfully.

"Who did it, then?" asked Donald.

"Well," Matt signed slowly, "it couldn't have been Larry or the other boys because they were all asleep and besides they wouldn't. . . . I think it was—"

"You think it was Abdul?" Donald finished for Matt.

"Right!" Matt nodded his head firmly for emphasis.

"Because of the red bandanna?"

"Yes," began Matt. "Abdul probably climbed down the tree like we did and lost it."

Whop! Donald felt a wad of warm, wet paper against his neck.

"Oh, yuk!" he said disgustedly as he peeled off the gooey mass.

Whop! Whop! Whop! More wads of paper smacked Donald and Matt. Matt looked over and saw the boys from his dorm with wide grins on their faces.

"Let's just say we're even after the surprise attack with the pillows," signed Larry with satisfaction.

"Even?" asked Matt. *The battle has just begun,* he thought. Matt began to tear a piece of paper from his notebook.

Just then Mr. Benning walked into the classroom with Saleem at his side.

"Get enough sleep last night?" he signed to Matt and Donald.

Donald and Matt nodded sheepishly.

It was like Mr. Benning not to be severe with the boys for their late night offense. Mr. Benning was the most popular teacher and dorm counselor at the school. He seemed to understand the mischief the boys often found themselves in.

"What kind of crazy clothes does he have on?" asked one boy as he pointed to Saleem's clothes.

"Looks like he still has on his pajamas!" Larry laughed.

"These are not pajamas!" retorted Saleem angrily. "For your information, dumbbell, this is my native dress from Pakistan. It's called *quameec-shalwar*," he fingerspelled this last word. "Men wear this all the time in Pakistan."

"Sissies!" one boy signed as he turned his head away from Saleem and the teacher.

"Come on now, let's show a little respect for things that are different from ours," Mr. Benning coaxed. "I want you to have a more open mind about these matters. I asked Saleem to talk to the class about his country today. And that included wearing his native costume." Mr. Benning pulled down the huge wall map in front of the classroom. "See? Here's Pakistan. China is to the north. India is to the east, and Afghanistan and Iran are to the west and northwest."

Whop! Whop! While he was signing with one hand and pointing to the map with the other, Mr. Benning's attention was directed to the map. Donald felt another spitball pelt him on the head. But before he could locate his attacker, Saleem began to sign and all attention shifted to him.

"My country became independent from India on August 14, 1947," he began.

40

"Is that like our Fourth of July?" asked a girl with glasses who sat toward the back of the classroom.

"Yes, that's right. And Pakistan's Muhammad Ali Jinnah, the man who founded Pakistan, is like your George Washington."

"What does Pakistan look like?" asked a boy. "Is it all green like Kentucky?"

"Some parts of it are," answered Saleem. "But Pakistan has mountains and a desert and is on the Arabian Sea."

"Can you body surf there?" asked Matt.

"Of course!" answered Saleem with enthusiasm. "You can do that and swim and sail and all sorts of other water sports."

"What language do you speak?" asked Mr. Benning.

"My family speaks Urdu," answered Saleem. "It looks like this." Saleem wrote on the blackboard:

"That looks weird," Ted signed. "I have never seen anything like that before!"

"What does it say?" asked another boy.

"It says, 'My name is Saleem Sheikh.' It's a little like Arabic and comes partly from the language called Hindi," Saleem explained.

"Do you go to church?" asked a girl.

"No, we go to the mosque and pray," answered Saleem. "We are Muslims. That's a different kind of religion than Christianity." Saleem paused. "Do you want to see some pictures from my home?" he asked.

"Oh, yes," replied several children with enthusiasm. They all got up from their seats and circled around Saleem.

"Here are some of my favorites," signed Saleem. "This was taken last summer at the beach. And here I am riding a camel along the sands!"

Many of the kids were gathered around Saleem. Matt got hit in the cheek with another spitball. He made a face and signed to Donald, "We need to declare war!"

"Hey, look what I have!" Donald said as he reached into his pockets and pulled out a handful of rubber bands. The boys grinned at each other. "They're left over from Susan's paper route," Donald explained. "I thought they might come in handy! You know what I mean!"

"Yeah," replied Matt with a knowing look on his face, taking a handful of rubber bands from Donald's palm.

By a stroke of luck, another teacher called Mr. Benning to the hallway. While the other kids were looking at Saleem's pictures, the boys loaded up.

Matt looped a rubber band around his index finger and over his thumb. He aimed at Larry and fired. *Zap!*

"Ow!" yelled one boy as he rubbed his sore

shoulder. He rolled some paper, stuck it in his mouth, and spit.

Whop! Zing! Zap! Whop! Rubber bands and spitballs flew around the room.

"Ow!" yelled Larry.

"Got yah!" Donald exclaimed.

For five minutes the battle went on. Soon the room was littered with wads of soggy paper and rubber bands.

Suddenly a flashing light and a ringing bell signaled the end of the class. The kids quickly grabbed their books and headed for the door.

"Hey, what's going on in here?" signed Mr. Benning, looking at all the rubber bands and spitballs on the desks and the floor.

"Gotta run to gym class," explained one girl as she ran out the door.

"Got shop in the vocational building and I'm late!" explained Ted as he, too, ran out of the classroom.

The kids managed to get past Mr. Benning with a quick excuse.

"Invite me to your class anytime," Saleem signed as he stood smiling in front of the teacher. "I like it here. Much more fun than in school in Pakistan!"

"Whew! Saved by the bell," signed Matt to Donald as they ran through the hallway.

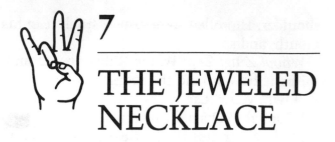

7

THE JEWELED NECKLACE

"**A**s a special treat," began Mr. Benning, "we're going on a field trip this afternoon."

The kids cheered and stood up in their seats. They were all excited to break the routine of the school day and leave campus.

It was Donald's third day at the deaf school and he was feeling a bit homesick for his mother and father, and even Susan. He looked out the window and daydreamed. *I wonder what Merlin is doing now,* he thought, wishing he was back in his bedroom cuddling his pet. *Is my treehouse okay?* he wondered, gazing at the Kentucky countryside.

"Donald . . . Donald!" said Mr. Benning as he gently tapped the boy's shoulder. "Do you want to join us?"

A big tear rolled down Donald's cheek. He quickly wiped it away. He didn't want the other kids to see him crying. "Yes," he replied. "I . . . I . . . I guess so." Another tear followed the first one down his face.

"He misses his family," Matt signed to Mr. Benning. Matt and Donald were close friends. Matt knew Donald missed his family because he missed his family, too.

"Why don't you call them from the dorm when we get back from town this afternoon?" suggested Mr. Benning. "That will make you feel better."

Donald's face brightened.

"We're going to the Danville College Library," Mr. Benning explained. "We will see a cultural exhibition of tapestries, paintings, and jewelry from Pakistan and India. This trip fits in nicely with Saleem's talk yesterday about his country."

Saleem was the last one on the bus. He was in another class and had to be excused. "Mr. Benning," signed Saleem. "My aunt and uncle will meet us at the library and guide us on the tour. They're history professors at the college and know all about this stuff."

"Great," replied Mr. Benning.

Fifteen minutes later, the school van pulled into the library parking lot. Saleem's Aunt Saba and Uncle Bill were waiting on the steps of the library. Saleem greeted his aunt and uncle.

"Do we have an interpreter?" asked Saba.

"I'm the interpreter," a young woman replied and stepped forward.

The group entered the library and the room where the exhibition was being held. The walls were hung with paintings and tapestries. Artifacts from Pakistan and India were in glass cases around the room.

"See those tapestries on the wall?" Mr. Benning

signed and spoke. "They must be hundreds of years old."

"Yes, they are," replied Saba. "They're from India and tell the history of the land now called Pakistan," she explained. The students watched the interpreter as Saba answered Mr. Benning.

"I wish I were rich and could have all those golden bracelets!" signed one girl.

"Ahhhh," exclaimed several girls, looking at a necklace displayed in its own case. The necklace rested on black velvet and glittered with many jewels.

"I like this best!" signed a girl.

"I see a diamond," Ted pointed to the glistening gem.

"And there's a ruby, and a sapphire, and an emerald," signed another girl. "What are those other jewels?" she asked.

"Those are a cat's eye, an aquamarine, turquoise, pearl, and coral," Saba answered. "This necklace has special historical significance because of the nine jewels. It's the most valuable piece in the exhibition."

"One, two, . . ." One boy began to count the jewels. "Nine. That's right, I counted nine," he signed enthusiastically.

Saba smiled. "That's right. You will find nine jewels on that necklace. They stand for the nine ministers who sat in the court of King Akbar, an Indian Muslim leader in the early sixteenth century."

"Wow!" exclaimed the children. "That was a

long time ago," added one girl.

"Indeed, it was!" replied Bill. "Pakistan is a country rich in history."

"I have seen that necklace before," signed Saleem. "I saw it at the museum in Karachi where I grew up."

The boys and girls turned toward Saleem. They were impressed with all that he knew and all the traveling he had done. Donald and Matt beamed with pride. After all, Saleem was *their* friend.

The students, Mr. Benning, Saba, and Bill walked around the exhibition a while longer, then headed back to the van. Mr. Benning thanked the interpreter. Saba took her nephew aside and asked him how school was going.

"Most of the time I like it," the boy replied. "But it hasn't been easy. Some of the boys pick on me."

"Well, just keep trying," encouraged Saba.

"Many thanks for the tour," said Mr. Benning to Saba and Bill as Saba and Saleem rejoined the group standing by the van.

"Our pleasure!" Saba smiled. "And, Saleem, will we see you this weekend?" she asked.

"No, no, not this weekend," answered Saleem. "Remember, we're all going to Cumberland Falls State Park for a camping trip."

"Oh, that's right," his uncle replied. "The weekend after, then."

The tired boys and girls filed into the van and plopped onto their seats. Saleem was the last one on the bus. As he walked down the aisle, Larry stuck out his leg. Saleem tripped and fell face forward to the floor. Larry and his friends began to laugh.

"Knock it off!" Mr. Benning signed angrily. "Larry, you will be punished for that. Come sit by me. And apologize to Saleem, right now."

Mr. Benning made a quick head count. He continued to lecture the boys and girls. "You kids have got to learn to be more tolerant of different kinds of people," he started in. "Larry, your hostility toward Saleem is not acceptable."

"But he looks weird and acts weird, too," Larry retorted in a nasty manner.

"Enough, Larry," said Mr. Benning. Frustrated with Larry's actions and attitude, Mr. Benning sank into his seat.

After supper that night, Ted tried to get together enough boys for a game of baseball.

"Where's Saleem?" asked Donald when he and Matt were playing catch.

"I don't know. Maybe he's tired from the trip to the library this afternoon," answered Matt. "Not to mention feeling bad after what Larry did to him. I haven't seen him since we got back."

"I didn't even see him at supper," Donald added.

Later, the boys lay on their beds reading comic books. Ted came running up the stairs and into the room.

"Matt! Matt! Donald! Donald!" Ted jumped up and down to get their attention.

"What is it?" asked Matt.

"Someone broke into the Danville College Library. That jeweled necklace—it's gone! I saw it on the captioned news," he signed. Ted was out of breath and his hands waved all around. "The police are looking for the thieves now. And there's a big reward for any information about the robbery!"

"Are you sure?" questioned Matt. "I don't believe that!"

"Where's Saleem?" asked Ted. "Maybe he knows something about all of this."

"I don't know," Matt answered.

"Yeah, I bet I know where he is," sneered Larry, who was standing in the doorway watching Ted's conversation with Matt and Donald. "He's probably helping the crooks get away with the stolen necklace."

Matt jumped off his bed and put up his fists. "Now you watch who you are accusing," he signed angrily, defending his absent friend.

"Saleem wouldn't do that!" Donald said quietly to himself.

"Well, he seemed to know a lot about those jewels at the library this afternoon," accused another boy standing next to Ted.

"And there he is." Larry pointed an accusing finger at Saleem as he walked into the room.

"What's up?" asked Saleem as he plopped down on his bed and picked up a comic book.

"Where have you been?" Matt asked.

"Yeah," joined in Larry. "A lot of people want to know."

"I have been . . . around," Saleem signed evasively. His brown eyes shifted quickly to the floor. He pushed a wavy black lock of hair to the side of his forehead.

"So where have you stashed the jeweled necklace? Sneaky foreigner!" accused Larry in a nasty way.

"Yeah," agreed several of the other boys.

"What necklace?" asked Saleem innocently.

Wanting to defend his friend, Matt explained. "Saleem, Ted saw on the news tonight that someone stole that necklace we saw this afternoon just as the exhibition was closing—about four o'clock."

"And you think *I* did it!" Saleem retorted angrily. "Well, you're all crazy!" Saleem's eyes welled up with tears.

"We're calling the cops and collecting the reward," replied Larry. "Let's go, guys!" He summoned the other boys and they stomped out of the room.

"Honest, I didn't do it," Saleem signed. "I didn't do it," he repeated and began to cry softly. Saleem plopped down on his bed and buried his face in his hands.

"Look, Saleem," Matt gently nudged his friend, "I believe you."

"I believe you, too," Donald agreed.

"But, Saleem," signed Matt, "if you don't tell anyone where you were, people are going to ask you questions because you have been gone since classes were over."

"I just can't tell you right now. Please trust me. Please?" pleaded the frightened boy desperately.

"Well, if you didn't do it, then someone else did, and we will just have to find out who," signed Donald.

"The Flying Fingers Club can solve this case." Matt smiled confidently.

"The Flying *what* Club?" questioned Saleem. He sat up in bed and wiped the tears from his face. Sharing with Matt and Donald made him feel better.

"It's a club we started," explained Matt. "We solve mysteries. Just last spring we found the thief who stole Susan's newspapers."

"Who's Susan?" inquired Saleem, getting more interested by the minute.

"She's my sister," replied Donald. "You will get to meet her this weekend at Cumberland Falls. Her Girl Scout troop is camping there."

Saleem pushed his wavy hair aside again and heaved a sign of relief.

"I wonder if this has anything to do with the attic?" Donald asked the other two boys. "Do you think it's connected in any way? And what about the red bandanna we found in the pine tree? It must belong to Abdul. Maybe he's connected with the robbery in some way. What do you think?"

"No, I don't think Abdul had anything to do with it," Saleem interjected in a forceful manner that surprised both Matt and Donald. "He's really a nice man. I know he wouldn't do anything like . . . like steal what doesn't belong to him. When I was with him, he told me—" Saleem stopped abruptly and put his hands in his lap. "Oh, never mind," he signed.

"So you were with Abdul?" questioned Matt.

"*Never mind,*" repeated Saleem emphatically.

"Wait a minute," Matt tried to reason with Saleem, "we're on your side. We only want to help. If you keep secrets then we can never get to the bottom of this."

"I just can't tell you right now," Saleem answered hesitantly. "Maybe later. Anyway, it's not what you think. It has nothing to do with the robbery. I know nothing about it."

Donald threw up his arms in exasperation.

No matter how hard the boys tried, Saleem would not tell them where he had been or what he was doing.

In a tumbledown cabin surrounded by evergreens in the woods near Cumberland Falls sat three men. It was midnight. A short, puffy-looking, red-faced man with a beard and cropped hair stared intently at a piece of paper. He abruptly looked up and said, "We have to move quickly."

"Keenan, we're trying to get the necklace out of here as fast as we can," Jack said impatiently. "Abdul has hidden the necklace in a good spot. We just have to wait awhile. Right now, the cops have all the roads going out of the county blocked. If we moved now, we would be caught for sure. Everything's under control. And," he said as he rubbed his hands together and chuckled, "who would ever suspect that we would hide the necklace in a dorm full of deaf kids?"

"Say, why don't you get that deaf boy from Pakistan to help you?" added Keenan, turning to Abdul who, until now, had been silent.

"No," replied Abdul in a strong voice. "Leave the kids out of it."

"But, he lives in the dorm and—"

"Look," Abdul interrupted, "I agreed to help you get the necklace and get it out of the country. The kids don't get involved."

"Okay, okay," Kennan relented. "Now, explain again about how you hid the necklace."

Abdul began to talk. "One of my jobs this month is to clean out the attics in the children's dormitories. When you gave me the necklace after the robbery, I went up to the attic in the boys' dorm and—"

8

AT THE FROSTY FREEZE

Next day, the news about the robbery quickly spread around the school. Some of the students, especially Larry and his friends, accused Saleem of stealing the necklace. At dinner in the cafeteria, even Ted ignored Matt and Donald and Saleem. The three boys played catch for a while after dinner, waiting to see if the other boys would show up to play baseball.

"Who cares about them!" Matt signed impatiently. "Let's go get a milkshake at the Frosty Freeze."

"Can we?" asked Donald.

"Sure," Matt replied. "We can walk down to the corner as long as we're back before dark. It will be light for another hour or two."

At the Frosty Freeze, Matt ordered first. "A strawberry shake," he said to the girl, using his voice and no signs.

"Huh?" asked the girl behind the counter with a startled expression on her face. Matt repeated his order, using only his voice.

The waitress turned to the manager beside her.

"This is my first day on the job and I don't understand that kid," she said nervously.

Seeing all the commotion and confusion he had caused, Matt turned bright red. Donald felt very badly for his friend.

Matt angrily grabbed the pencil on the counter and wrote down his order on a pad of paper. He threw several quarters on the counter and turned away in disgust.

Matt got his milkshake and sat down. When Donald and Saleem joined him at the table, he was still fuming.

"They're so dumb," he signed, slurping his milkshake. "Why do they always have to make a face when I talk? I hate that."

"Maybe they don't understand your speech," Donald signed, trying to be helpful.

"My speech is fine!" retorted Matt. "My speech teacher at school says so. And she always gives me an A on my report card," he added with emphasis.

"Can you understand Matt's speech?" Saleem asked Donald.

"Well . . . er . . . um . . . sometimes. But really the signs help a lot," Donald replied, trying to smooth over the situation.

"You hearing people are all alike," accused Matt, looking straight at Donald and shaking his finger. "You only understand things when you want to!"

"Look, Matt, don't get mad at me. I'm on your side. I was only trying to help and—"

"Oh, just forget it!" Matt gulped his milkshake.

Donald, his feelings hurt, turned away from the boys at the table. He noticed some men sitting at a table by the window. "Look over there," signed Donald to the other boys. "Isn't that Abdul?"

"Where?"

"Sitting over there with those two bearded men," Donald replied. "I wonder what they're talking about?"

Abdul drummed his fingers on the table. Then he gnawed his nails and scratched his chin. The short red-faced man motioned to Abdul and the other man. They all got up and walked toward the exit, looking back at the boys.

"What's that all about?" Donald was feeling a bit scared by the angry looks of the men.

Abdul entered the restaurant again. Avoiding eye contact, he walked toward the boys and handed Saleem a note.

"What does the note say?" both Donald and Matt asked after Abdul left.

Saleem slowly read the note. Then his face turned white. "Ahhh!" he gasped fearfully.

9
CRACKING
THE CODE

"**H**urry up and tell us!" Donald demanded nervously.

But Saleem did not sign a word. He just stared intently at the piece of yellow paper in his hand, his face drained of color. Saleem showed the note to the boys.

اپنے دو ستونوں کو میان بہر مت جانے دو ورنہ تم سب خطرے میں پڑ جاؤ گے۔

"I can't understand this!" signed Matt impatiently. "What does it mean?" He nudged Saleem.

"It's written in Urdu," signed Saleem.

"We *know* that!" Donald was exasperated. "Translate it for us! And hurry!"

"Yeah," agreed Matt. "Tell us what it says."

Saleem hesitated. Finally he signed, "It says, 'You and your friends stay out of the attic or something terrible will happen to all of you!' "

Donald gasped and put his hand over his mouth. His stomach jumped into his throat and his knees felt like jelly.

Matt was angry, not scared. "What a jerk! So it is Abdul and his friends who are using the attic. Who are they to tell *us* to stay out of *our* attic? What nerve!"

Donald's initial fright had passed. "Maybe the note is more of a warning than a threat. Maybe Abdul is trying to protect us."

"I don't understand it," Saleem signed. "I thought he was my friend. We even—" Saleem abruptly stopped in the middle of his sentence.

"You even what?" questioned Matt.

"I don't want to tell you." Saleem put his clenched hands in his lap.

"Saleem!" Matt signed with an annoyed look on his face. "How can we help you if you don't tell us all the facts. Stop keeping secrets! Trust us!"

Saleem looked at Matt. Then he looked at Donald. He began to think that maybe he should trust these boys. After all, they had defended him from the other boys. What loyalty Matt and Donald had shown him! He decided to open up.

"Well, Abdul invited me to his apartment and he showed me all of his watches. He has hundreds of them. All different kinds. And lots of little tools. Screwdrivers and everything."

Matt started signing before Saleem was finished. "Watches, huh! So he steals watches as well as jewels!"

"I don't think he did it," signed Saleem slowly and thoughtfully. He gazed back down at the note he held in his hands. "I have a feeling that Abdul is in trouble and that he can't help it. He started to tell me about missing his family and everything. I just think that something else is going on." Saleem looked down at the note again. "Hey," he signed excitedly, "there's some writing down here that I can't quite make out. It's in English and it's smeared at the bottom of the page." Saleem held the note up to the light trying to decipher the letters on the yellow paper.

"Well, at least we know that Abdul doesn't live in the attic," signed Matt.

"Yeah," replied Donald, "but he must have been up there for some reason besides just cleaning it out."

"To hide something?" Matt guessed. "Like all the watches he stole."

"Or the necklace," signed Donald slowly. "That's it. I bet the jewels are there." Donald was excited. "We need to go back up there and look for them. Maybe the necklace is stashed behind some of that old dusty furniture."

Saleem was still peering at the paper. "I think one word is 'umber' but I can't make out the other one."

" 'Umber' is not a word," signed Donald.

"Maybe it's 'number.' " Matt was thoughtful.

"I just can't make it out," signed a frustrated Saleem.

"Umber, umber, umber," repeated Matt. "It makes no sense to me."

As the boys walked back to the school, they repeated over and over, "umber, umber, umber." But none of them could figure it out.

After the boys returned to the dorm, Matt suggested they investigate the attic one more time.

"Let's wait until everyone goes to bed," signed Matt secretively.

A few hours later, the three boys crept out of their beds and into the hall. Matt went to get the ladder. Once again, the three boys climbed the ladder, pushed up the trapdoor, and hoisted themselves into the attic.

The boys looked and looked. They could find no evidence of any watches or the necklace.

"Look at that picture. Over by the window," Matt signed to Donald and Saleem.

"So what?" answered Donald.

"That picture wasn't by the window when we were here before. It was against the wall. Remember?"

"Oh, yeah," answered Donald. He admired how observant Matt always was.

"Someone was up here," signed Matt.

"Do you think it was Abdul and those other men?" asked Saleem.

"We need more evidence to say for sure," Matt answered. "But whoever it was, they moved the picture."

"I wonder why? There are so many unanswered questions in this case," signed Donald. "I hate to admit that we need a girl's help, but Susan might have some ideas."

"We will see her tomorrow at Cumberland Falls. Maybe she can make sense of all these clues," replied Matt.

"I want this old picture in my room," Matt decided. "I like it. Help me, will you?"

The boys carefully slid the painting through the trapdoor and down the ladder. Matt put the painting against the wall behind his bed. "I can hang it up later," he signed to the boys.

The boys slipped back into their beds without being discovered. Almost before Matt's and Saleem's heads hit their pillows, they were fast asleep, exhausted from their late-night sleuthing.

Donald was restless and tossed and turned in his bed. He dozed on and off, never falling completely asleep. Finally, just as he was falling asleep, he thought he saw a shadowy face at the window. The sharp blade of a pocketknife slit the window screen and a man crawled into the dorm room. Was he awake or asleep? Donald wasn't sure!

10
CUMBERLAND FALLS

Donald woke up abruptly. "Whew!" He sighed with relief as he looked over at the window. The screen was intact and had not been slit. What a nightmare! He thought, *That sure was scary. Did I eat something awful before I went to sleep last night? Mom says eating too many sweets causes nightmares.*

"Come on, boys, off to breakfast and then we will pack up the van for our trip to Cumberland Falls," Mr. Benning signed as he entered the dorm room. "Matt, I need to talk with you. What's this?" Mr. Benning had spotted the painting by Matt's bed.

"Oh, I found it around . . . in one of the closets here," answered Matt vaguely. "I thought it would look neat on the wall. Kind of historical and all that."

"Kind of historical?" replied Mr. Benning. "Matt, do you know who this is?"

"No," answered Matt.

"Thomas Hopkins Gallaudet. He started the first school for the deaf in Hartford, Connecticut. We talked about him in class, remember?" Mr. Benning explained.

"Oh, I forgot," answered Matt. "But what's the painting doing here?"

"Who knows?" replied Mr. Benning. "Maybe someone gave it to the school years ago and it was mistakenly stored away." He ran his fingers down the side of the frame. "Matt, this painting might be worth something. I think we should notify the superintendent and see what she thinks."

"But can I keep it until then?" asked Matt. "It will look great on the wall."

"Yeah," interjected Donald, "especially next to Superman."

Mr. Benning looked thoughtful. "I guess it would be okay. Now, Matt, I'm really concerned that a lot of the boys are not accepting Saleem—and Donald, too. I know they're led by Larry and I've dealt with him the best way I know how. Maybe you could talk to the boys when you're playing ball or just messing around."

"I will try," said Matt as he shook his head. "But I think it's hopeless," he added.

"Just try, Matt. It's important. Now, hurry up and let's get going. The day is slipping away from us."

By the middle of the morning the boys had packed and loaded everything in the van. Soon they were riding down the highway, whizzing past rolling fields filled with grazing horses. It was a wonderful, bright, sunshine-filled day to go camping at Cumberland Falls!

"Remember all the safety rules we went over," Mr. Benning lectured while the van bumped over the road into the park. "Cumberland Falls can be dangerous. The river currents can sweep you away before you know it. The rapids are beautiful but dangerous. And fires . . ." he went on and on.

Donald didn't think Mr. Benning would ever stop. If he had heard it once, he had heard it a million times—"Don't hike or swim alone" and "Don't leave any fires unattended." He knew all that stuff. He gazed out the window. It sure was beautiful up here in the woods. Most of the leaves on the trees were still green, but he noticed patches of yellow here and there. The steady hum of the van was comforting. He daydreamed.

The van pulled up to the lodge and the twelve boys jubilantly jumped out. A piney smell filled the air. It was cool in the woods, but still comfortable enough for shorts and T-shirts. Mosquitoes swarmed about, but no one seemed to mind. No one except Saleem.

"Ow! Ow! Ow!" Saleem yelled as he smacked the bugs on his legs. "This is just awful. I wish I hadn't come. Where's the bug spray? I need it quick. Will someone *please* get me some bug spray?" He went back to slapping his legs and arms.

"Just calm down, Saleem," said Mr. Benning as he tried to console the Pakistani boy who was not used to camping in the woods. Here's the bug spray. Soon you will forget about the mosquitoes and really enjoy yourself." Mr. Benning patted the boy on the back and headed for the lodge.

"What's that over there?" asked Donald, catching Mr. Benning's attention. Donald pointed to a stone bridge.

"Oh, that's a natural arch. It's a bridge made from sandstone. Those structures are quite common here. We can hike over it once we get settled in at the lodge."

Matt watched two chipmunks fighting over some acorns under a giant oak tree. They scurried around and around then shot up the tree. The boys were excited and ready to go exploring.

"Boys," Mr. Benning ordered. "Bring all your gear inside. On the double!"

A piece of paper was tacked up on the front door of the lodge. *What's this?* he asked himself as he read the note.

"Donald! Donald!" Mr. Benning called. "Donald, here's a note for you. It's from your sister."

Donald ran up to the door and read the note. "Susan and her Girl Scout troop are here," he explained to Mr. Benning. "They're camping about a half mile up the road. Susan wants Matt and me to go horseback riding. Can we go, Mr. Benning? Can we go?"

"As long as you unpack and make up your bunks first. I had planned to take all of you on a hike this afternoon, but there's plenty of time for everything. Why don't you take Saleem along, too? If he can ride camels, I'm sure he can ride a horse! We will hike up to the Girl Scout camp with you."

"Yippee!" Donald jumped in the air.

Mr. Benning greeted the Girl Scout leader while Susan ran towards Donald and Matt.

"Donald," called Susan, "please interpret for her. I don't know enough signs yet."

Donald didn't mind Susan being bossy this time. He could show off his signing skills. All eyes were on him as he interpreted. Donald loved the attention. He felt so proud of himself.

"Donald," said Susan's scout leader, "tell Mr. Benning that we have been practicing some songs in sign language so we can have a sing-a-long and a sign-a-long tonight."

"And guess who taught them?" boasted Susan. Donald rolled his eyes.

Mr. Benning liked the idea and invited the girls to come to the boys' lodge that night. He then headed up the trail with the other boys.

Susan and several of her friends, Donald, Matt, and Saleem walked to the corral to pick out their horses.

"Susan, I have to tell you what happened," whispered Donald to his sister as they saddled their horses. He explained all the strange incidents that had taken place at Matt's school.

"You mean you got stuck in the attic?" Donald nodded.

Susan was jealous. She wanted in on the adventure, too.

"I don't understand about this Abdul guy. If Abdul is the janitor, then he's supposed to be up in the attic. I mean, that's what janitors do. They clean attics, basements—things like that. So what's the big deal about him being up there?"

"Susan," said Donald impatiently, "he was up there at night! All we *really* know is that someone stole that jeweled necklace and everyone is blaming Saleem!"

"The Flying Fingers Club needs to get the necklace back," replied Susan.

"But how?" said Donald slowly.

By now, the Girl Scout leader and the other kids had headed up the trail leaving Susan and Donald, deep in conversation, behind. Susan looked up and saw that the other kids had left.

"Donald, we better talk later. Let's get going."

Several minutes later, Donald was still trying to get his horse to move.

"Come on, Donald, hurry up! You're so slow!"

"I can't get this horse to move, Sue!" Donald was frustrated. "He just won't go."

"Kick his side," Susan advised. "Hard!" By now the other riders had disappeared up the trail.

Donald kicked and yelled "Giddyap," but his horse would not budge.

"Golly, Donald!" Susan exclaimed impatiently. She rode over to an oak tree and broke off a small branch. She approached Donald's horse from the back and swatted it with the branch.

Heee—Heee! The horse neighed, arched its neck, and reared up on its hind legs. The horse neighed again and took off up the trail like a shot, with Donald holding on for dear life.

"Oh, what have I done! What have I done!" gasped Susan. She saw only the dust that Donald's horse had kicked up on the trail.

I'm going to kill you, Susan, thought Donald, gritting his teeth. His horse took off in the opposite direction from the other kids. Trees whizzed by. Donald pulled back on the reins. "Whoa! Whoa! Whoa, horsey!" he yelled. But the horse kept going. Donald's heart was pounding so loudly he could feel it in his head.

Finally they came out of the woods into a green, grassy pasture. The horse unexpectedly and abruptly stopped in front of a small, clear pool of water. The horse neighed softly and lowered his head to drink. Donald gratefully slid out of the saddle, his sneakered feet landing at the edge of the pond. He clutched his sides and breathed deeply, sinking down to the soft grass. After a few minutes, he rolled over on his back and let out a loud gasp of relief. *That wasn't so bad. Kind of fun, really,* Donald thought, proud of his bravery.

Looking up into the sky, Donald noticed a stream of black smoke. *Must be a cabin nearby,* he thought. *Maybe they can help me find the way back to the lodge.* He got up, brushed the grass and twigs from his shorts, and walked through the trees. The horse seemed content slurping the cool water. Donald decided not to get back on that horse until he absolutely had to.

As he approached the cabin, he saw three men near the cabin door. *It's Abdul!* he exclaimed to himself. *What's he doing here? And the two men from the Frosty Freeze!* Donald sneaked close enough to hear the conversation, but was careful to hide behind the bushes so he wouldn't be seen.

"What do you mean, you can't find the necklace?" Keenan angrily demanded of Abdul.

"I hid it up in the attic in the picture frame, like I told you," explained Abdul. "When I went back to get it, the picture was gone."

"How do we know that you're not trying to double-cross us?" the red-faced Keenan accused Abdul.

"Why would I do that? I want to see my family," Abdul responded.

Donald could not understand what Abdul's family had to do with it. He wished Matt and Susan were here to help him figure out what was going on.

"I think he's telling the truth," Jack, the taller man, said.

"I don't care if he's lying or telling the truth!" threatened Keenan, pulling on Abdul's collar. "Get that necklace fast! Bring it up here to the cabin by tomorrow night. Understand?"

Donald was amazed. *We had the necklace all the time and we didn't even know it!*

A twig snapped under Donald's foot. He froze. His heart stopped. Donald quietly sank into the bushes.

"What was that?" Keenan asked loudly. "I thought I heard something."

"Oh, it's just a squirrel. Calm down!" Jack said scornfully.

"I will go back to the school now," said Abdul sadly, "and try to find the picture."

"Yeah, you better, if you know what's good for you and your family," retorted Keenan. "We will be waiting for you tomorrow night. And, Abdul," he cautioned, "don't try to double-cross us!"

Donald quietly got up and raced back to the clearing. *Now what am I going to do?* he thought, leading the now contented horse away from the pond. *I'm lost in the woods!*

Donald looked over his shoulder to make sure he wasn't being followed. He mounted the horse and, to his surprise, the horse started at an easy pace back the way they had come. The horse, familiar with the area, was heading home. "Well, you're all right after all! Guess you were just thirsty," Donald spoke aloud as he hugged the horse's neck.

What do we do next? he thought. *Blow the whistle on the thieves? But we don't have any real evidence. Only what I overheard. And what about Abdul's family? Will Abdul find the picture by Matt's bed?* His mind was racing. In no time, Donald and his faithful horse made it back to the corral.

Susan was waiting for him. "Donnie," she exclaimed, "are you okay? Where have you been? I was worried about you!"

"We have more worries than you think, Sue," he said as he dismounted.

11

AROUND THE CAMP FIRE

Donald explained to Susan what had gone on at the cabin in the woods as they walked back to Donald's lodge. "This Abdul guy is in deep trouble," Susan said. "Maybe he's being set up."

"What do you mean?" asked Donald with a puzzled look on his face.

"Well," explained Susan. "Maybe he was forced to steal the necklace but he really didn't want to."

"Why? To save his family?" replied Donald.

"I don't know," added Susan. "It's just hard to say at this point. We need more clues to figure out the whole story."

"Oh, there you are!" signed Matt as he walked out of the lodge and saw Donald and Susan talking under a tree. "Glad you got back okay, Donald!" Matt grinned. "I got stuck doing potato peeling duty tonight. Yuk!"

Susan began signing to Matt. She was slow and awkward. Donald was impressed, though, that his sister was trying. Matt smiled knowingly at Donald.

"Matt," Susan signed, "we think the necklace

will be here at Cumberland Falls tomorrow night."

Donald could not hold his hands still any longer. "The necklace is in the picture frame!"

"The necklace is right by my bed in the dorm this very minute?" Matt looked questioningly at Donald. "We had it all that time?"

"Sure did," Donald assured Matt. "We have got to clear Saleem's name. This is our chance to prove he didn't have anything to do with this!" added Donald.

"Why are they against Saleem?" asked Susan.

"Because he knew a lot about the jewels and the necklace came from Pakistan. That's where he was born," explained Donald.

"And because he was missing when the robbery happened. He won't tell anyone where he was," Matt added.

"But the boys in the dorm were against Saleem from the very beginning, even before the robbery. They just don't like people from other countries —or even hearing people," signed Donald.

"Well, the Girl Scouts have had no problem. All the boys from the school seem to like us." Susan smiled innocently.

"That's because you're *girls*." Donald was disgusted. "And some of those boys are *stupid* enough to like girls."

Swish, swish went Susan's ponytail. "Oh, Donald," she said with a superior air, "when will you ever grow up!"

"Do you think we should call the police about the crooks?" signed Matt, changing the subject.

"The crooks may be too dangerous for us to handle alone."

"No, I think we should try to nab the thieves ourselves. The newscaster on TV said there was a reward. We could use the reward money for our club," signed Donald with enthusiasm.

"Yeah, we could put an addition on the treehouse," Susan signed awkwardly. Donald and Matt both frowned at this idea.

Susan began to take over as usual. Donald rolled his eyes. "Okay, here's the plan, boys," she began. Donald interpreted for Matt. "We can sneak away from the lodge tomorrow night and go up to the cabin in the woods. If we can get—"

"Yeah," interrupted Matt, "by then Abdul will be back from the school with the necklace."

"We can wait until the crooks are asleep and then sneak into the cabin and get the necklace. Then we can run back here and turn them in to the park rangers."

"And collect all the reward money," Donald added with a big smile. "Yippee, I can't wait."

"Gotta go now," signed Susan, as her eyes shot down to her watch. "I'm on chow duty tonight. We're making chili. See you guys about eight o'clock tonight. I will be back here with the Scouts."

"For signing songs around the camp fire?" asked Donald.

"Yep," replied Susan. "We have been practicing 'My Old Kentucky Home' for three whole weeks!"

That evening, fifteen Girl Scouts poured into the

boys' camp. Mr. Benning had lit a bonfire in the middle of the camping area.

"Why did you boys leave your hearing aids in the lodge?" he asked.

"Don't want the hearing girls to see them," replied one boy.

"Yeah," signed another boy. "We want to impress the hearing girls."

After about ten minutes, the kids began to relax with each other. Susan's efforts at giving her friends a crash course in sign language had paid off. Some of the girls were trying to fingerspell and sign to the boys.

A bright full moon lit the sky and the air became cooler. The kids sat around the bonfire toasting marshmallows and drinking hot chocolate.

The girls began their program. They signed several traditional songs and some favorite Girl Scout songs. After the songs, some of the boys told the girls their favorite jokes. Donald did his best to interpret.

"Ahhhh!" yelled Saleem. "I can't keep my marshmallow on the stick. It keeps falling into the fire!"

"Those are the best ones. When you pull them out, they're all burnt and gooey. They're delicious! Here, I will show you," signed Donald. He helped Saleem retrieve his marshmallow from the fire. "Have you seen Susan? I have been looking all over for her."

"Not since they finished singing and signing," replied Saleem.

Donald wanted to find her to see what time they should meet the next night to go to the cabin in the woods. He looked and looked. Donald finally spotted Susan and three other girls near the front door of the lodge. They were giggling. One girl was holding her sides she was laughing so hard. *I wonder what's going on!* Donald thought. He shrugged his shoulders and returned to the camp fire. He would catch up with Susan later.

Everyone had a good time that night. The tired Girl Scouts and their leader piled back into their van. Several girls signed parting messages to the boys.

One girl flashed the *I love you* sign.

"See you tomorrow," signed another girl.

The kids had planned to meet again the next evening for volleyball at the girls' camp.

"Sweet dreams!" signed Susan. When she signed this message, three girls in back of the bus cracked up with laughter.

Donald was suspicious. He was angry with Susan because she was so busy with her friends that he had not gotten a chance to talk to her about tomorrow evening. And Susan was up to something. He knew his sister only too well. Susan loved to play pranks on him.

When the boys walked into the lodge, they were in for a big surprise.

"Hey! What's all this toilet paper doing here?"

White streamers of toilet paper criss-crossed the beds, furniture, and the light fixtures.

"It looks like a New Year's Eve party,"

laughed Mr. Benning when he saw the mess.

"What's this?" asked another boy.

A note was taped to the mirror. The note said, "Beat the boys in volleyball!" Another note nearby said, "Girls will win!" And still another note read, "Tomorrow you lose!"

"We will show those silly girls," signed Saleem. "We will beat *them* tomorrow night."

"Yeah," agreed Larry. "We're stronger than they are."

Mr. Benning raised his eyebrows. He was surprised that Larry and Saleem were at last agreeing with each other. Their wish to beat the girls in volleyball had somehow smoothed over their conflict. At least temporarily.

But that wasn't the end of the boys' surprises. When Donald got into bed, the sheets were cold—and "crunchy." The more he moved, the more the bed "crunched."

"Oh, yuk, what's this stuff in my bed?" Ted asked.

"It's in my bed, too," Matt answered.

"Mine, too!"

"Same!"

"It's corn flakes under the sheets!"

That night the light stayed on until well past midnight. The boys plotted their revenge.

"The girls will be sorry!" signed Larry, beating his hands Tarzan-like against his chest.

12

THE BOYS' REVENGE

"Since Saleem can't eat sausage, I will take his," signed Larry as he forked several links off the platter in the center of the table. The boys were seated in the lodge dining room eating their breakfast.

"You're such a pig," signed one boy.

"I'm a growing boy," Larry signed right back, glowering.

While several of the boys still considered Saleem and Donald to be outsiders, the tension in the group was lessened because of the distractions at the camp. Donald and Matt were so wrapped up in solving the mystery of the missing necklace that they avoided any conflict with the other boys.

"What time are we going to the Girl Scout camp?" asked Saleem.

"Oh, we will leave about seven o'clock after we have eaten supper," answered Mr. Benning, gulping his coffee. "Volleyball is on the agenda for this evening."

"Hurry up with the breakfast dishes, boys," Mr. Benning prodded. "Let's not waste any more time inside. The great outdoors is waiting for us."

That night the boys arrived at the girls' camp. The volleyball net was set up on the grassy field. The children chose teams and began to play.

"I wonder why the boys haven't mentioned the mess we made in their rooms," one girl asked Susan as she swatted the volleyball across the net.

"Beats me!" replied Susan. She bent down to tie her sneaker.

The boys just seemed cheerful and happy to be outdoors playing. They had planned to act as if nothing had happened the night before.

"Something's going on," said Susan to one of her friends. "It's not like Donald to go without saying something."

Donald pulled Susan to the side during a break in the volleyball competition. "We have got to go up to the cabin tonight to try to get that necklace," he whispered.

"Oh, Donald, we're only one game behind and it's my turn to serve," she replied. "Let me just play the next game, then I will go with you." And she turned away to join her teammates.

"Sue," Donald grasped Susan's arm, "this is much more important."

"Yes, I know it's important," said Susan. And Donald saw that she made the sign for *important* correctly for the first time ever.

"But, just let me play one more game," Susan insisted. "We want to beat you boys!"

Donald was disgusted with his sister. She always got her way even though they needed her now to go up to the cabin. He was furious! "Just forget it," he angrily snapped at his sister.

Donald grabbed Matt and the two boys disappeared into the woods. Susan wasted no time in returning to the volleyball court.

Meanwhile, a couple boys were busy in the girls' lodge. They sneaked in the back door with a large sack of metal pots and pans.

When the girls opened the door that night, the pots and pans clanged to the floor. String, strung from every doorknob to every bedpost, blocked their entrance. The girls stood with their mouths open in amazement. On the mirror was a sign that read, "Ha Ha! We got you!".

13

AT THE CABIN

Matt and Donald made their way from the girls' lodge to the river. "The cabin is about two miles from here, close to the river," signed Donald. "That's my guess."

The boys followed the moonlit trail that Donald's horse had galloped up the day before.

"Ah!" screamed Donald and stopped short.

Matt bumped into him and signed, "What is it?"

"I thought I saw a wild animal," replied Donald, calming down. "It's probably a squirrel or something like that."

"I think it was your shadow," Matt signed, grinning. "Are we lost? We have been walking forever."

"No, we're not lost," answered Donald. "This all looks familiar to me. I don't think the cabin is too far from here."

Matt began to jump up and down when he spotted the cabin. "See the trucks parked in the driveway?" He pointed excitedly.

"That must be them!" Donald answered. "We have to be careful. They might have guns or something."

"Let's go!" Matt was bursting with excitement. "I'm tired of Saleem getting blamed for the robbery. And there's a reward. We'll be heroes if we catch the thieves!"

The boys tiptoed through the pine needles in the clearing and up to the cabin window. "I can't reach," signed Matt. Because he was short, he frequently had difficulty reaching things. "I hate being so short!"

Donald found cut logs on the side of the house and dragged two of them over to the window. Matt helped him prop the logs against the side of the cabin. The boys stepped up on the logs and held onto the window sill for balance.

The boys peered into the window. Abdul and Jack and Keenan were sitting at the table.

"Here's the money we promised you for hiding the necklace," Keenan said gruffly to Abdul. "Now hand it over." Abdul opened a soft cloth bag and turned the sparkling necklace over to the men.

So Abdul found the picture in the dorm room and got the necklace, Donald thought.

"Ah!" exclaimed Jack to Keenan. "This is a real prize! It will bring a good price on the black market," he said as he fingered the necklace. The nine jewels gleamed.

"Yeah, I should have been paid more for hiding it!" Abdul complained.

"Listen, Abdul, a deal is a deal!" Keenan shook his fist and scowled at Abdul. "Besides," he went on. "The other half of the deal is that your family will be over here soon. We have made all the arrangements. They will be leaving Pakistan tomorrow."

All the time, Matt was nudging Donald to sign to him what the men were saying. Donald was straining so hard to hear the conversation that he leaned too far into the screen. With one arm on the window sill for balance and the other hand trying to form signs, he found himself in a very awkward position. Suddenly, he lost his balance. Matt reached over to grab Donald, but not soon enough. Both boys fell off the logs and rolled into the tall, unmowed grass.

Thump! The top log hit the solid ground.

"What's that?" shouted Jack. "What's that noise?" He ran out the cabin door. By now the boys had gotten to their feet and were rushing for the trail. They made it halfway to the woods before Jack caught them.

We're dead ducks! thought Donald gloomily.

Jack grabbed the boys by their collars and marched them back to the cabin where Keenan and Abdul stood in the front yard.

"I have got the two kids who have been snooping around," he said with a laugh.

"You boys are just too nosy for your own good," snapped Keenan.

"Uh, er, uh, we're lost from our camp," said Donald with a quivering voice.

"Sure, kid, do you think we're dumb enough to believe that?"

"We don't know anything," repeated Donald. His knees shook with fright.

"Now what? What are we going to do with these two kids?" Jack asked.

"We can't let them go. If we do, they will tell the cops," Keenan replied slowly.

Matt was scared and confused. He looked to Donald to interpret for him but Donald was too frightened to form any signs. The boys shivered with fright.

Abdul stepped over and sat down on a log. "Let the boys go," he said emphatically. "One of them is deaf. When they're discovered missing, every police officer in the country will be looking for them."

The three men began arguing among themselves about what to do with the boys.

"Throw them in the river!" Jack suggested.

"Let them loose in the woods. That will give us time to escape," said Keenan.

A streak of lightning suddenly lit up the sky. *Crack!* Thunder and rain followed.

"Everyone to the cabin," bellowed Keenan. "We have to decide what to do with these kids and then get out of here quick."

Matt thought fast and kicked his sneaker off.

"I think maybe a swimming accident," Jack suggested.

"Yeah, like they were out at night and they lost their balance on a rock and hit their heads and fell in!" added Keenan. Jack and Keenan laughed. Abdul didn't even crack a smile.

Will we get through all this alive? Donald wondered frantically.

Inside the cabin, Jack opened a beer for each of the men and passed them around. They sat talking while the frightened boys lay on the couch. Donald attempted to sign to Matt what was happening, but his hands were shaking so hard and he was so scared that he found himself forgetting all his signs. Even though the boys were exhausted they could not go to sleep.

Suddenly, a long black snake slithered across the cabin floor.

"Snake," called out Donald in a panic.

Abdul pulled out his knife and threw it at the snake, but he missed. The snake continued to crawl across the floor straight towards Matt. Matt jumped up off the couch and ran across the room. The men got up from their chairs and started after the snake, which was heading for the bedroom.

The boys seized the opportunity and ran for the door.

"Hurry! Hurry!" signed Matt to Donald.

"Hey, you boys. Get back here," Keenan yelled, stopping them at the door. "Next time, instead of letting Abdul kill it, we will let the snake get you," he chuckled.

Rain continued to pound on the side of the cabin. Miserably, the boys turned back and slumped on the couch.

14

WHITE
WATER
CHASE

Susan stood behind a pine tree in the pouring
rain watching the cabin. "Yuk!" she exclaimed
as water dripped down her jeans. Susan wondered
what all the commotion was. By the time she had
arrived at the cabin she had been able to see the
men through the cabin window, but not the boys.

What's that? she said to herself as she spied a
dirty sneaker in the mud puddle. *Must be
Donald's or Matt's,* she thought. Ideas ran wildly
through her head. She knew the boys must be in
trouble. She felt guilty about joining them so late.
If only she hadn't insisted on playing that last
game of volleyball! And the boys had won anyway,
by one game! Now, Donald and Matt were in deep
trouble. *What should I do?* she wondered
desperately. She was getting wetter by the minute.
Deciding she had better go back for help, she
pulled out her jackknife and made a large X on the
tree. *I can at least let the boys know that I have
been here,* she thought.

In the cabin the boys were feeling doomed. It
seemed hopeless. Donald had stopped interpreting

so Matt had to rely on speechreading and facial expressions. He could not understand much.

"Hey, Keenan," said Jack. "We have got to get out of here. Those kids will be missed soon and there will be search parties. I'm getting worried."

"Yeah, I know," answered Keenan. "Let's tie up the kids, get the raft out, and escape down the river. We can hitch a ride when we get out of the county. I think that's about ten miles south of here. We can't chance driving on these roads. They will be crawling with cops."

"But, Keenan," Jack exclaimed, "those rapids are pretty rough, especially when we get around the falls. With all this rain the river will be high. It's dangerous, especially in the dark and the rain!"

"You want to go to jail for the next twenty years?" Keenan retorted.

"No!"

"Well, then, let's go! Tie the kids up and gag them. Get the necklace."

"Let the boys go!" insisted Abdul. "Robbery is one thing but kidnapping is *really* serious. I don't want anything to do with it!"

"We worked hard setting this job up. And you're not going to stop us now. After we sell the necklace, we will be set for life. You, too. You got your cash. I don't want this all ruined just because of two lousy kids. Now, come on!" Keenan grabbed the bag with the necklace in it.

Once outside, the boys were quickly herded to the river. They did not see Susan's X on the tree. The men shoved the two boys into a thick rubber raft with a small motor on the back. Donald wished he could have interpreted the men's conversations to Matt, but his hands were tied!

Suddenly Donald had an idea. The boys were sitting back to back so Donald moved his hands over to the side so that his right hand touched Matt's hand. He tried to fingerspell on top of Matt's hand, but his fingertips barely reached. He was getting more discouraged by the minute.

The thunderstorm had turned into a soft steady rain. Droplets of water danced on the river as the raft moved downstream with the current.

Susan had made her way back to the lodge. By now, the two boys had been missed and the police had been notified. Mr. Benning was extremely upset.

"If I had only kept an eye on those two! I should have stopped them from leaving," he criticized himself harshly.

Several police officers stood around the distraught teacher and Susan, trying to understand what had happened.

"It's about the necklace in the picture frame in the attic. Donald and Matt knew the thieves were bringing the necklace to Cumberland Falls," Susan explained.

"What necklace?" asked one police officer.

"What attic?"asked another man in a uniform.

"Hold it!" exclaimed another officer. "Will someone please explain to me what's going on?"

"Oh!" exclaimed Mr. Benning, who was picking

up most of the conversation through speechreading. "Do you mean the stolen necklace from the library?"

"You mean the one Saleem stole!" interjected Larry who was standing in the background.

"I did not," signed Saleem forcefully.

"Until we get some interpreters here, we're completely lost," said one police officer, a bit annoyed with all he was missing. I'm going to phone back to headquarters to send someone."

"At this time of the night?" questioned another officer. "You will never find one."

"I can sign a little bit," Susan said.

Slowly, the story became clear.

Back on the river, the group had been traveling for about twenty minutes through the smooth water. The rain had stopped and now mosquitoes were swarming around the men and boys in the raft. Matt couldn't swat the mosquitoes since his hands were tied. He was working himself into a frenzy because of the mosquitoes. He tried to call out but the gag in his mouth stopped him. Angrily, he stood up and with all his might he started pushing and shoving with his shoulder.

The three men in the boat were busy trying to navigate the raft. "Hey, stop that kid," Jack called.

Keenan reached over to grab Matt and push him to the bottom of the raft.

Suddenly the raft tilted to the left and cold water gushed in.

"Hold the raft!" yelled Abdul. "Lean to the right!"

"Look ahead," shouted Jack. "Rapids!"

"We will have to go over it," shouted Abdul. Suddenly the raft hit a rock, then careened over the rapids. By now the boys were drenched. Initially the water was refreshing, but now they were cold.

"Hey!" yelled Abdul. "Made it through that one!"

The river forked. To the left was the waterfall.

"Steer to the right!" yelled Abdul from the front of the raft. "We don't want to go over the falls."

"What?" shouted Keenan.

"I said steer to the right." The thundering noise of the nearby waterfall made conversation nearly impossible.

Keenan started the raft's motor and all three men began paddling furiously to head the raft away from the falls.

Despite their efforts, the raft continued toward the waterfall. The men began to panic. Luckily, the raft hit a rock and veered to the right away from the falls.

"Whew!" Keenan exclaimed as he steered the raft down the river. "We made it!" The three men relaxed, but not for long. Saved from the falls, they faced another danger.

Up ahead was a clearing in the woods. Suddenly, several bright spotlights shone on the raft.

"This is the police!" bellowed a man with a bullhorn. "Give yourselves up!" On the shore stood four uniformed police officers and Susan.

"We're going through," yelled Keenan, opening

the motor as far as it would go. The raft sped by the police. The police hopped into their motorized rubber raft and took off after the thieves and the captive boys.

In the commotion, Matt managed to loosen the ropes tied around his hands just enough to grab the bag holding the necklace and the satchel containing Abdul's money and throw them overboard. The satchel opened and green bills spread out on the top of the water. The necklace sank out of sight.

"Hey," called out Jack. When he saw what Matt had done he reached over to grab him but Matt ducked. Jack lost his balance and fell back into the raft.

"Oh, no!" yelled Abdul.

The raft was caught in an eddy of water and spun around and around. The bottom of the raft scraped on a submerged jagged rock. The rock sliced the bottom of the raft, which began to fill with water.

"Ah! Ah!" yelled Jack as he fell overboard, clutching an oar.

"Help, help, I can't swim," yelled Keenan.

Abdul reached over and cut the ropes from the boys' hands. The boys landed in the water and grabbed the side of the raft to stay afloat. Donald and Matt pulled off their gags and gasped for breath.

"Swim, boys!" Abdul called to them. "Get over to the shore!" Abdul motioned frantically towards shore.

But Matt did not swim to the shore. He took a deep breath and quickly dove to the bottom of the river in search of the necklace.

Donald looked over his shoulder for his friend. He saw the white of Matt's socks as he disappeared under the water. A wave lapped over Donald's head and he swallowed a mouthful of the muddy brown water. Donald began to gag. He turned over on his back and floated. The water carried him swiftly downstream. He spit out the water and gulped in the night air. Doing the sidestroke, he made his way to shore. When he got to the bank, he stuck his feet in the mud on the river bottom and pulled himself up by grabbing onto a tree branch that hung over the water. He was so weak that he had to try several times before he got on dry land. He rolled over on his back to catch his breath. Suddenly, he remembered Matt.

"Matt, Matt," he yelled. "Forget the necklace! Get over here!" Donald yelled and yelled in a wild frenzy. That Matt was deaf and underwater did not stop Donald from yelling. He began to cry. "Hey, you stupid jerk! Do you hear me? Come up! Come up!" Donald looked up the river and he looked down the river but he could not see his friend.

Donald heard police car sirens and soon the shore was covered with uniformed officers. The police in the raft had caught up to the crooks and brought them to shore. But still Matt did not appear.

"Oh, Donald," cried Susan, who had led the

police to the cabin, "I'm so happy you're safe!" She hugged him.

"But what about Matt?" sobbed Donald uncontrollably. "Where is he? Why hasn't he come up?"

"Son," consoled a police officer in a gentle voice. "We will do our best."

Tears streamed down Donald's mud-streaked face. "You have got to find him. You hear me? Find him!" Donald collapsed to the ground in hysterics.

15

MISSING
LINKS

Several police officers stood on the shore flashing their lights into the river. "Any sign of the boy yet?"

"Nope. Haven't seen anything."

"Take a few people and go to the other side of the river. Maybe he's on the other shore," said Lieutenant Dayton to an officer.

Men combed the woods and shore looking for Matt. An hour went by and still Matt had not been found.

"The scuba divers are on their way," said Lieutenant Dayton to Susan. "It's pretty deep here in the middle of the river. And the current, well, it's strong."

It was a glum group that lined the shore. Donald, bundled up in blankets, sat in a police car. Even though the adults pleaded with him to leave, Donald refused.

"I don't want to leave," he said.

"But you would feel better if you went to the hospital," argued the police officer.

But Donald would not listen. He was waiting for Matt.

"The scuba divers are here," someone said. The two divers put on their wet suits and other equipment and jumped into the cold water. They disappeared quickly beneath the muddy brown water.

After about ten minutes, they emerged. One of the divers took off his mask. "It's so dark and muddy we can't see a thing. Even with these underwater lamps, it's just impossible. I think we had better wait until morning and start the search again."

The Lieutenant had one last idea. "Get those flares from the trunk of the car," he said. "If the boy can't hear us, maybe he will see the lights of these flares. He may be lost in the woods."

The police lit the flares, which rocketed up and slashed the sky with yellow. After a few minutes, the men shot off more. Then more. But still no sign of Matt.

By now the search party had returned from the other side of the river.

"Not a trace," said one officer despondently.

The group was steadily losing hope. They waited for a while before leaving the river bank. Donald was chewing his nails in the car. He had stopped shivering, but fear still enveloped him—the fear of losing his best friend. Susan was on the river bank talking with the officers.

Suddenly, they all heard a rustle in the bushes.

"What's that?" called one of the officers.

Matt emerged from the woods. He was covered in mud from head to toe. Around his neck was the jeweled necklace.

Donald jumped out of the police car and threw off his blanket. "Matt!" screamed Donald. "We thought you had drowned!" he signed.

"So did I," Matt answered.

Susan scrambled up the river bank and ran towards the muddy boy. "What happened? What happened?" she cried excitedly. "Are you all right?" she signed.

"I got swept downstream in a fast current after I found the bag with the necklace on the bottom of the river," answered Matt. "Lucky for me, it carried me into shore." Matt collapsed on the ground, exhausted.

The lieutenant bent down to feel his pulse. "You okay?" he asked Matt.

Matt just looked at him.

"We better take Matt and Donald to the hospital and have them checked over," said Lieutenant Dayton.

"Would you turn on the siren and the flashing light?" Donald requested as he climbed into the police car after Susan. The boys sat in the back with their arms around each other.

The next morning, Matt and Donald returned to the lodge. They explained to Mr. Benning and the boys what had happened.

"We have to go down to the police station this afternoon and answer some questions," Matt finished the story. "Saleem, you have to go with us. And Susan, too."

"Don't forget to bring the note that Abdul gave us at the Frosty Freeze," Matt instructed Saleem.

"I just don't understand it," began Donald. "Abdul really saved our lives. After all, he was the one who cut our ropes. We would have drowned. If he were really part of the crime ring, he wouldn't have helped us so much."

"And I'm sorry that Saleem was accused by some of you boys of something that he didn't do," added Mr. Benning.

Larry responded, "He's not off the hook yet. There are still some unanswered questions."

"Knock it off, boys! Right now!" Mr. Benning was as angry as the boys had ever seen him. No matter how hard he tried, it was impossible to change some of the boys' negative attitudes toward the boy from Pakistan.

There was a pause. Then Mr. Benning continued, "Matt and Donald, you need to take it easy this morning."

That afternoon Donald, Matt, Susan, and Saleem were sitting in Lieutenant Dayton's office. The jeweled necklace on the policeman's desk was clean and sparkling.

"Tell me about this Flying Fingers Club," he said as he sipped his coffee. Susan immediately started explaining. Donald and Matt rolled their eyes. Even though they were grateful that Susan had come to find them and called the police, they still resented the fact that she had stayed for that last volleyball game. They could have been killed if the crooks had decided to do away with them at the lodge!

"Abdul signed a confession last night," the Lieutenant began.

Donald started interpreting for Matt and Saleem.

The Lieutenant continued. "Abdul and his wife and baby are from Afghanistan. He's a jeweler and watchmaker by trade."

"That explains why his room at the school is filled with watches," Matt signed as his quick mind began to sort out all the details.

"But why did he come all the way to Kentucky to steal *one* necklace?" asked Saleem.

"This necklace," began the detective as he picked it up and slowly fingered it, "is worth a quarter of a million dollars because of the jewels and its historical significance. It's a prize any dealer or museum director in the world would like to have."

"Oh, my gosh!" exclaimed Susan. "I would love to wear it to school for just one day! Wouldn't the girls be impressed!"

"Anyway," continued the lieutenant, "Abdul and his wife and baby escaped to Pakistan because there was a war in their country. When he was in a refugee camp, he met some men who were part of a group of international art thieves. The crooks promised Abdul that, if he helped them steal this necklace, they would move Abdul and his family to the United States. Abdul's part in all this was to hide the necklace. He wasn't with Keenan and

Jack when they stole it. Abdul waited in the woods behind Catfish Pond for the other two to give him the necklace."

"But why go to all that trouble? Why hide the necklace in the picture frame in the dorm attic?" asked Matt.

"These art thieves are smart and well organized," explained the detective. "They knew we would have road blocks out after the robbery. So they decided to hide the necklace at your school until the pressure was off. And then move it out of the country."

"That is, until the Flying Fingers Club wrecked their plans," smiled Susan. Donald and Matt looked at one another and rolled their eyes again. Saleem was noticeably upset. He began to cry softly.

"What's wrong?" asked Matt. "Are the boys at the lodge still picking on you?"

"I don't care about them!" signed Saleem angrily. "But I do care about Abdul. I don't want to see him go to prison. We prayed together and—"

"So that's where you were on the afternoon of the robbery," interrupted Matt. "You were praying with Abdul."

"Yes," answered Saleem as he dried his eyes. "It's our custom for the men to pray together."

"Honestly, Saleem!" scolded Donald. "It took you long enough to tell us!"

"I didn't tell anyone because I didn't want the boys to make fun of me anymore. I have had enough of their teasing," retorted Saleem.

Thoughtfully, Saleem continued. "I met Abdul when I was walking down by Catfish Pond before dinner. We went to his apartment . . . and prayed. He talked about his family . . ." Saleem's face had a faraway, sad expression. "He must have had the necklace with him the whole time we were together!" Saleem finished.

"Oh, what about the note? Won't that help Abdul?" Saleem's face suddenly lit up. He reached into his pocket for the note and showed it to the lieutenant.

Donald explained. "Abdul warned us to stay away. He just didn't want us to get hurt. That's Urdu writing. Saleem can translate it for you. And this faint part in English says 'umber.' We didn't understand at first, but we think Abdul was warning us about Cumberland Falls, too."

"Hm," said the detective as he scratched his head. "With Abdul's confession and the evidence you kids gave us—well, I can't promise you anything but I will make sure the judge knows these facts. It may lighten his sentence some. Abdul said in his confession that he shut you boys in the attic to scare you so that you wouldn't get hurt. That ties in with the warning note. We'll have to wait and see. Don't get your hopes up, though."

Susan broke the silence that followed the lieutenant's statement. "What about our reward?"

"Yes, you kids deserve the reward the Danville Art League set up to help find the necklace. I will make sure you get it."

"But make the check out to me!" Donald said emphatically. "I'm the president of the club, you know."

Matt nodded his head in agreement.

"I don't recall any elections," Susan said.

"Susan," Donald answered impatiently, "be quiet!" Susan glared at Donald as she swished her red ponytail.

"We did it, Donald," Matt signed proudly. "We found out what was happening in the attic and we cleared Saleem's name."

Donald just grinned at his friend.

On the way back to their campsites in the police car, Susan began to tease Donald. "Guess who's going to be the boss of the house for a whole week?"

"What do you mean?" asked Donald.

"Well," Susan explained, "I wasn't supposed to tell you, but Mom has to go to a soils conference in California over Thanksgiving break and I get to take care of the house. That means I'm boss," she added emphatically.

"Mom will miss my birthday. It's during Thanksgiving vacation this year," said Donald. He was disappointed. He was not looking forward to Susan bossing him around.

"I think Mom is planning to take you with her. Oh, golly!" she said as she clasped her hand over her mouth, "I hope I didn't spoil the surprise!"

A big smile spread across Donald's face. He wondered what plans his mother was making.

ORIGAMI